EMMA'S RULES 4 A DADDY

1) He cant be 2 old

2) He cant be 'fraid of the dark or thunders

3) He should maybe like kissing my Mom sometime

4) He's got 2 like dogs—big, big dogs, and homwork
   and snowbal fights and especiallee chokolot chip
   coookees

5) He's got 2 like kids—especiallee ME!!!!!!

Dear Reader,

In this season of giving thanks, there's only one thing as good as gathering with your family around the holiday table—this month's Silhouette Romance titles, where you're sure to find everything on your romantic wish list!

Hoping Santa will send you on a trip to sunny climes? Visit the romantic world of La Torchere resort with *Rich Man, Poor Bride* (SR #1742), the second book of the miniseries IN A FAIRY TALE WORLD…. Linda Goodnight brings the magic of matchmaking to life with the tale of a sexy Latino doctor who finds love where he least expects it.

And if you're dreaming of a white Christmas, don't miss Sharon De Vita's *Daddy in the Making* (SR#1743). Here, a love-wary cop and a vivacious single mother find themselves snowbound in Wisconsin. Is that a happily-ever-after waiting for them under the tree?

If you've ever ogled a man in a tool belt, and wanted to make him yours, don't miss *The Bowen Bride* (SR #1744) by Nicole Burnham. This wedding shop owner thinks she'll never wear a bridal gown of her own…until she meets a sexy carpenter and his daughter. Perhaps the next dress she sells will be a perfect fit—for her.

Fill your holiday with laughter, courtesy of a new voice in Silhouette Romance—Nancy Lavo—and her story of a fairy godfather and his charge, in *A Whirlwind…Makeover* (SR #1745). When a celebrity photographer recognizes true beauty beneath this ad exec's bad hair and baggy clothes, he's ready to transform her…but can the armor around his heart withstand the woman she's become?

Here's to having your every holiday wish fulfilled!

Sincerely,

Mavis C. Allen
Associate Senior Editor

Please address questions and book requests to:
Silhouette Reader Service
U.S.: 3010 Walden Ave., P.O. Box 1325, Buffalo, NY 14269
Canadian: P.O. Box 609, Fort Erie, Ont. L2A 5X3

Daddy in the Making

SHARON De VITA

SILHOUETTE *Romance*®

Published by Silhouette Books

America's Publisher of Contemporary Romance

 SILHOUETTE BOOKS

ISBN 0-373-19743-8

DADDY IN THE MAKING

Copyright © 2004 by Sharon De Vita

This edition published by arrangement with Harlequin Books S.A.

® and TM are trademarks of Harlequin Books S.A., used under license.
Trademarks indicated with ® are registered in the United States Patent
and Trademark Office, the Canadian Trade Marks Office and in other
countries.

Visit Silhouette Books at www.eHarlequin.com

Printed in U.S.A.

SHARON DE VITA,

a former adjunct professor of literature and communications, is a *USA TODAY* bestselling, award-winning author of numerous works of fiction and nonfiction. Her first novel won a national writing competition for Best Unpublished Romance Novel of 1985. This award-winning book, *Heavenly Match*, was subsequently published by Silhouette in 1985. In 1987, Sharon was the proud recipient of the *Romantic Times* Lifetime Achievement Award for Excellence in Writing.

Sharon met her husband while doing research for one of her books. The widowed, recently retired military officer was so wonderful, Sharon decided to marry him after she interviewed him! Sharon and her new husband have four grown children, five grandchildren, and currently reside in the Southwest.

Chapter One

The jangling of the telephone barely broke through Lieutenant Michael Gallagher's haze of fatigue and exhaustion. But when the telephone kept ringing, one hand slid out from under the covers and snatched it up. "This better be good—*very* good—or you're dead," he snarled.

"Gallagher, it's Commander McKenna."

"Sir?" Michael's mind immediately snapped to attention at the sound of his commander's voice.

"Gallagher, did you snatch a toddler out of the path of a speeding truck yesterday afternoon?"

Yesterday afternoon?

Rubbing a hand over his darkly stubbled face, Michael swore under his breath. The stress from working undercover for six months trying to close down a major drug-dealing operation had taken its toll. He was exhausted and nearly burned out. He could barely remember his name let alone what had happened yesterday.

Yesterday seemed a million miles and memories away.

Frantically, he tried to think, to remember what had happened yesterday afternoon.

He'd finally closed out his case. His suspects were in custody, his reports were done and he'd headed home for his first decent night's sleep in six months.

Then he remembered the toddler. And almost swore again.

"Yes, sir." Michael had to clear his throat. "I did. The mother was distracted. Talking on her cell phone. The kid just darted into the street after his ball. I happened to be standing right there, saw what was happening and reached the kid before anyone else could. It was no big deal, sir."

"That's where you're wrong, Gallagher. Apparently, the press thinks it's a very big deal. Your picture is all over the front page of every major newspaper in Chicago."

"What?" Michael said, bolting upright in bed.

"Your picture, it's all over the papers this morning," the commander repeated with waning patience. "A reporter just happened to be passing by and captured you in the act, holding the toddler out of harm's way. Now I've got a very nosy reporter cooling her heels in my outer office wanting an exclusive interview with Chicago's latest hero cop. You've been dubbed the Sexiest Cop In The City, Gallagher."

"Damn," Michael growled, gripping the receiver tighter and shaking his head in mortification.

"My sentiments exactly, Detective." It wasn't hard to hear the derision in his commander's voice. "Gallagher, I'm sorry, but I've got no choice. I'm putting you on thirty days' mandatory leave—with pay—effective immediately." The commander ignored Michael's sputtering protests.

"Maybe by then, this story will die down and the press will lose interest in you. I can't have one of my best undercover cops compromised by having his face splashed all over every damn newspaper in the city. It could jeopardize your life as well as any investigation you're involved in."

"But—"

"Thirty days' leave," the commander barked. "Starting right now, Lieutenant. Understand?"

"I understand," Michael said grimly, dragging a hand through his black hair.

"And Gallagher, do us all a favor. Get outta town. This reporter is not going to stop digging until she gets what she wants. I figure you might have thirty, maybe forty-five, minutes before she tracks you down at home. I want you far away and out of her reach until all this nonsense dies down, do you hear me?"

"I hear you, I hear you." Michael snapped the covers back and was already dragging his weary body out of bed. He reached for his jeans, still crumpled in a heap where he'd stepped out of them yesterday.

"I'll see you in thirty-one days."

"Yes, sir," Michael said glumly, as he stepped barefoot into his jeans, dragged them up and did up his zipper.

"Oh, and Gallagher?"

"Sir?"

"Try to keep your nose clean and your face out of the newspapers until then."

After spending nearly ten minutes muttering vicious imprecations about the Chicago press under his breath, Michael stuffed some clothes into a duffel bag and grabbed his laptop and the file of scrawled notes he'd been accumulating for almost ten years. Then he called his family to tell them what had happened and that he was heading out of town on vacation until the heat from the press died down.

Not that they wouldn't know. As the eldest son in a family of seven, he and his five brothers and one sister were incredibly close. Considering all his brothers were either Chicago cops or firemen, no doubt they'd *all* seen the morning papers.

It was a good thing he was getting out of town, Michael decided with a grim smile as he frowned up at the pewter sky before shoving his duffel bag and laptop into the back seat of his vintage Mustang. Otherwise, he'd never live down the razzing from his brothers and sister.

Sexiest Cop In The City, indeed, he thought in disgust. Fat white snowflakes dropped lazily from the cloudy sky as he pulled into the busy afternoon traffic.

He hadn't a clue where he was going. He was too tired to think, but the last thing he wanted was a confrontation with the press. So Michael drove along the busy city streets and then onto the interstate.

Somewhere between the Illinois and Wisconsin borders, the wind picked up and the clouds in the sky shifted and darkened, dropping more flakes of fat, fluffy snow. With the radio tuned in to a station softly playing oldies and the bucolic countryside rolling by, Michael let his thoughts drift and finally felt some of his inner tension ease.

Months of undercover work had taken their toll. Living on the edge, burrowing himself deep in the drug underground, always watching over his shoulder and always worrying about having his cover blown or his life taken had left him bone weary of the rat race of lies and deceit.

He loved being a cop. It was a Gallagher family tradition. His grandfather had been a Chicago cop and so had his father—until his father had been killed in the line of duty when Michael was barely eleven—so it had always been expected that as the eldest son in the family, he would join the force as well, which he'd dutifully done.

But he'd always harbored another dream, a secret dream he'd never had the courage to talk about or admit to anyone.

For ten years, he'd been accumulating notes on all of his cases and writing down interesting facts and incidents, hoping one day to weave all of his experiences into a book.

But he'd never had the time.

Until now.

The thought caused a buzz of excitement to race through him. He couldn't remember ever having a full month off before, a month just to do anything *he* wanted.

Lost in his thoughts, Michael drove farther away from Chicago, wanting to get far enough away from the city to avoid the press and also to avoid being recognized.

The temperature outside had dropped considerably. Without realizing it, he'd driven full tilt into the mouth of the winter snowstorm.

This deep into Wisconsin, the interstate had turned into a narrow, two-lane highway that looked as if it hadn't been plowed or salted in a couple of hours. But considering how hard and fast the snow was coming down now, it might have been only minutes since the highway had been plowed.

If he pulled off the interstate now, in the middle of nowhere, he might end up having to spend the night in his car. His battered leather bomber jacket and jeans didn't provide much protection from the elements and, with less than a quarter of a tank of gas in his Mustang, he would probably run out of gas long before morning and run the risk of freezing to death.

Michael decided to try to make it to the next town where, he hoped, he'd find somewhere warm to hole up for the night. He was relieved when he finally saw a sign for the next town. Chester Lake, Wisconsin, population: 1,275. Chester Lake was just eight miles ahead.

It took him almost thirty-five minutes to creep along the eight miles. He almost grinned with relief when he saw the Chester exit sign, immediately followed by a sign for the Chester Lake Inn.

Slowing to a near crawl, Michael carefully exited the interstate. He swore softly when he hit the end of the exit ramp and slid right through a stoplight, unable to halt on the icy, snowpacked road. Fortunately, there were no other vehicles around.

Turning left in the direction of the only visible lights that he estimated to be about a mile away, Michael turned off his radio and turned his heater up another notch.

Worried about how much gas he had left, Michael glanced down at his gas gauge for a moment and then looked up just as a white-tailed fawn limped onto the road right in front of him.

Instinctively, Michael swore as he hit the brakes and jerked the wheel, trying to avoid hitting the animal. Startled by the headlights, the animal pivoted and limped back where it had come from. The car fishtailed viciously and then slid in a circle before Michael lost control.

"Damn," he swore softly, trying to cushion his head and face for the blow as his car slammed into a frozen snowbank.

* * *

The dogs began to growl.

With a frown, Angela DiRosa glanced up from the guest registration book she'd been updating. "Mackenzie! Mahoney! Stop that growling," she scolded, glancing at the two mammoth malamutes who were sprawled in front of the large stone fireplace. "There's nothing to be afraid of. I told you, it's just the wind blowing," she said, tucking her long dark hair back behind her ear and grinning at the two dogs. "It's a storm, boys. Nothing you haven't seen before, so stop your growling."

"This is a bad one, Angie," her uncle Jimmy warned from his perch at the game table, where he was sipping steaming hot chocolate and playing a solitary game of checkers. "Worst of the winter so far." He glanced out the Thermopane windows that rose from floor to ceiling on either side of the soaring fireplace.

The howling wind had pushed the snow halfway up the windows and was blowing hard against the panes, making it nearly impossible to see anything in the distance. "Looks like it might keep up most of the night."

"I know," Angela said with a sigh, closing the registration book and coming out from behind the counter to give each of the dogs' heads a soothing stroke. "The weatherman said we could get up to thirty inches," she added with a worried frown.

She glanced at the roaring fire, checking the stacked wood to make sure there was enough to keep the fire burning through the night. With this kind of storm, they never knew when they might lose power. The fireplace in the large combination lobby/living room of the twelve-room inn wasn't there just for aesthetic purposes, but also for heat and light if necessary.

Rubbing her hands up and down her sweater-clad arms, Angela frowned when the dogs' growls grew louder and they rose to sniff and prowl at the large, locked front door of the inn.

"What on earth is wrong with you two?" she demanded as if a response from the dogs would be forthcoming. "Come away from that door and stop that growling."

"You hear something, Angela?" her uncle Jimmy asked with a sudden frown.

"I'm not sure," she admitted, feeling an unusual skitter of alarm. The inn was technically closed for the winter. It would only reopen for a week during the annual Chester Lake Christmas Festival, but that was still almost a month away—and as part-owner and manager of the inn, she knew they had no reservations until then.

In the six years since she'd divorced her husband and fled with her baby daughter to the comfort and security of her uncle's isolated inn in Wisconsin, she'd never felt really frightened or alone, probably because she'd been so grateful for the peace, quiet and comfort she'd found here after her tumultuous marriage and divorce.

She loved the quiet solitude and steady security of her life here. She'd finally found the peace she'd been searching for, as well as a safe place to raise her daughter. If loneliness was an occasional visitor, it didn't seem such a high price to pay for all the wonderful benefits she'd derived from living here.

But right now, it wasn't comfort she was feeling, but rather an odd bit of *discomfort,* almost a premonition, and she wasn't sure why.

"Sounded like a thump or a knock," her uncle added, reaching for his cane and slowly pulling himself to his feet.

She couldn't imagine someone foolish enough to be out

wandering around in this blizzard. In spite of her unease, Angela went to the front door, pushing the dogs back with her leg as she snapped open the lock and yanked open the door, letting in a rush of cold wind and a blast of icy snow.

"Oh my word," Angela said, reaching for the injured, all-but-frozen man in the battered leather bomber jacket who was leaning heavily against the door, bleeding from a head wound and covered in snow from the top of his head to the tips of his ridiculously inappropriate cowboy boots.

"Uncle Jimmy, come help me," she called, nudging her shoulder under the injured man's arm to give him something to lean on as she guided him inside and toward one of the large, overstuffed sofas in front of the roaring fireplace.

The dogs circled around her, growling softly at the stranger. She nudged them out of the way, keeping her attention on the injured stranger.

"Must be crazy," she muttered to herself as she helped the injured man down onto the sofa. "There's a blizzard out there," she said unnecessarily. Slowly, she lifted his legs up, noted his jeans were soaked and caked with snow and then carefully removed his snazzy, snow-filled cowboy boots, letting them drop to the floor with a thud.

With something else to focus their attention on, the dogs immediately began to growl and sniff at the stranger's boots.

"No, not crazy," the man sighed, wondering if he was delirious. He could swear there was an angel sitting next to him. A beautiful, dark-haired angel who smelled like heaven. He blinked again, not certain if he was awake or dreaming, conscious or delirious. He'd been walking for what seemed like forever, getting colder and colder until he couldn't feel any part of his aching body.

"Michael," he said, trying to smile but not quite able to

manage it. His lips, his face were too cold. "My name's Michael, not crazy."

"So you're a comedian, as well," Angela said with a shake of her head, amazed and amused that the man could joke when he was clearly frozen and in obvious pain. She frowned at his forehead, gently touching the still-bleeding wound. He winced and tried to turn his head away from her.

"Are you hurt anywhere else?" she asked softly, letting her gaze take him in as she quickly unzipped his leather jacket and carefully eased it off his shaking body.

He didn't answer; he merely lay quiet and shivering. She grabbed an afghan from its perch on the back of the couch and tucked it around him as she took another good look at him.

He had thick, rich ebony hair which was coated with snow. She wasn't quite certain of the color of his eyes, but his face, although red from the elements, was filled with sharp planes and angles, giving him somewhat of a rough-hewn, rugged look. His nose looked as if it had been broken once or twice; it still bore a slightly crooked scar at the bridge. His mouth was long, the lower lip slightly fuller than the upper lip, giving him a seriously sensuous look that would make any woman wonder what it would feel like to have those long, full lips on hers.

If she had to guess, she'd say it had been days—possibly weeks—since he'd bothered with a razor. The dark stubble of beard that covered his chin and cheeks gave him a slightly dark and dangerous look that only increased her earlier anxiety.

His face wasn't soft, she decided, feeling her nerves tighten, but it was definitely the kind of fascinating masculine face that would draw a woman's interest—and keep it for a good long while.

Disturbed by her own thoughts, Angela quickly shifted her gaze and silently scolded herself. She must really be feeling lonely if she was drooling over a mysterious injured stranger.

"Uncle Jimmy," Angela called. "Would you shut and lock the front door, then run into the kitchen and get the first aid kit and the extra blankets?"

With his cane clicking softly on the polished wood floors, Jimmy turned on his heel and headed back to shut and lock the front door, which was still wide-open. Snow was blowing in and chilling the room.

"I'm going to need some of your clean dry socks and flannel pajamas, as well," she added, before turning back to Michael with a frown. She didn't like the look of that cut on his forehead. While it wasn't particularly deep, it was swelling, and turning green and blue. Blood was still seeping slowly out of it. She wasn't certain if he had a concussion, but she was going to try to find out.

"Michael?" Gently, she shook his shoulder, felt the strength in it. "Michael, can you open your eyes and talk to me for a minute?"

She waited a moment while he struggled to open his eyes and keep them open. She flashed him a brilliant smile in encouragement.

"Good." She leaned over him to check his eyes. She wasn't a nurse, but his pupils appeared normal. He looked slightly dazed, but that was to be expected with a head wound. She touched the cut on his forehead again, relieved that it looked like the bleeding was stopping. "Is there someone I should call? Someone who's expecting you?"

Michael heard her, but it sounded like her voice was coming from down a long tunnel. He was so cold and every single inch of him ached and throbbed. Michael tried lifting a hand to touch his forehead.

"Don't touch your forehead yet," Angela said gently, taking his hand in hers and covering it with her other hand to warm it. "I've got to clean your wound. Now Michael, can you hear me? If you can, lift your other hand." She waited while he finally managed to lift his hand. She took it as well, and rubbed it between her own warm ones. "Good. Now is there someone expecting you? Someone who needs to be called?"

Michael thought for a moment, trying to remember. "No," he finally managed. "On vacation."

Angela nodded. "Okay, good. You're on vacation, so no one's expecting you tonight or will be worried, right?"

"Yeah."

"Did you have a car accident, Michael?" Angela asked gently, taking the blankets from her uncle's arms and wrapping them around Michael.

"Yeah. Lost…control trying not to…hit…an injured fawn. Right off the interstate exit."

"Was anyone else involved or in the car with you?" she asked quietly, stroking his cheek to warm it and to try to keep him awake.

Michael's eyes slid closed and he simply huddled under the blankets. "No… Alone," he finally said.

"Good. Good. That's very good, Michael." Gently, she stroked his cheek to encourage him and then flashed a smile. "Just a few more questions. Your forehead's bleeding, Michael. Are you hurt or bleeding anywhere else?"

"Dunno," he finally muttered with a scowl.

Angela swallowed hard. It had been six years since she'd been this close to a man, let alone touched one, but she really didn't have a choice at the moment. She had to find out if he had sustained any other injuries.

She hesitated for a moment, letting her gaze go over him again. He was what her late mother would have called one helluva specimen of a man. He was big, well over six foot four, she estimated, and had to weigh at least two hundred and twenty pounds. He wasn't fat by any stretch of the imagination, but he was broad chested, well muscled and incredibly well built.

No wonder her heart was all but tripping over itself. Thank God she was totally immune to men, she thought, trying to bolster her defenses, because if she wasn't, *this* was exactly the kind of man who could become a frightening temptation.

Hadn't her ex-husband been just such an intensely masculine man? A man who'd broken down her defenses and barriers with his lies and deceptions?

She'd been too young and far too naive and in love to even *consider* that the man she'd married had been lying to her. Not just about who he was, but what he did. He'd concealed his real name and occupation so she wouldn't know he was the son of a well-known criminal, and was now following in his father's illegal footsteps. By the time she'd discovered his deception, it had been too late. They'd been married for two years, and she'd been expecting his child. Still, disillusioned and pregnant, she filed for divorce.

It had been very difficult to forgive herself for being so foolish. Her only excuse had been that she'd been young and thought herself blindly in love—but she'd learned that you couldn't love something that wasn't real, and nothing about her life, her husband or her marriage had been real.

She was wiser now, she thought with a grateful sigh, and she would never again allow a man to betray or deceive her, nor would she ever put her heart at risk again.

Angela felt her pulse quicken and her stomach jitter as she quickly, but efficiently, ran her hands over Michael's finely sculpted muscles checking for injuries, trying not to think about what she was doing.

Her fingers tingled as they grazed over him, from his firmly chiseled shoulders to his narrow slim hips, and then from his ankles to his knees. She shook her head at the cold soggy jeans that were clinging to his skin.

She had to get him out of these cold, wet clothes, the sooner the better. Aside from his head wound, he didn't appear to be injured or bleeding anywhere else. She could only watch him tonight and pray he didn't have any internal injuries.

Right now, she was more worried about his body temperature, that he was perilously close to hypothermia.

While his leather jacket, designer jeans and fancy boots might be perfectly stylish, they were also perfectly stupid to be wearing for this kind of weather. If he had been from around here, he certainly wouldn't have wandered outdoors dressed like that in the middle of the worst storm of the year.

"Is he in shock?" Jimmy asked, peering down at the inert man cautiously as he handed his niece the first aid kit.

"I don't think so," Angela answered, laying a hand to Michael's stubbled cheek and turning his face to hers. "Can you open your eyes, Michael?" She stroked his cheek, her hand warm and soft against his icy skin. "Michael? Can you open your eyes?" she repeated softly.

"Yeah," he muttered, letting his eyes flutter open again, then immediately closing them as the overhead light seemed to burn through him. There was definitely an angel sitting over him, he decided. And as far as angels went, she was eye-poppingly gorgeous. He'd like nothing more than to just keep looking at her but he just couldn't seem to keep his eyes open.

"Left this on the doorstep," Jimmy said, setting down Michael's duffel bag, his laptop and a file folder on the coffee table in front of the sofa. "Fancy boots, skimpy leather jacket and designer jeans. City fella, definitely," he said with a dismissive sniff. "I'll go get some of the Christmas brandy. Give him a good snort. It should bring him around and warm him up." Limping off, Jimmy glanced back at Michael with another sad shake of his head.

Gently, Angela began to clean Michael's head wound, relieved to see that once the blood was cleared, it was a clean cut that wasn't deep enough or wide enough to require stitches. But from the way it had swelled and was bruising, he probably had one heck of a roaring headache. At her touch, Michael winced and groaned, trying to turn away from her.

"Easy, Michael," she soothed. "I'm just bandaging your wound. I'll be done in a minute." With quick efficiency, she carefully applied a butterfly bandage to his still-cool skin.

"Michael?" Angela touched his cheek again, trying to tempt him into opening his eyes. "I need you to drink this." Jimmy handed her a small glass half-filled with amber liquid.

"Michael, I'm going to lift your head and give you

something to drink to help take away some of the pain, okay?"

His eyes fluttered as she lifted his head with one hand, and held the glass with the other. Carefully, she tilted the glass, letting him sip slowly so he wouldn't choke. She managed to get the brandy in him before his eyes closed and he collapsed against the couch again.

He was beginning to warm up, he thought, nestling his face closer to the warmth and softness of the angel's hand. He must have dozed, because the next thing he knew, someone was helping him to his feet.

"Michael?" Angela tried to balance his weight against hers. "I'm going to take you upstairs and get you settled. Do you think you can walk?"

"My notes, my laptop," he muttered, trying to look around.

"They're in the living room, Michael. Don't worry about them or anything else. I've got everything you need. Come along now, Michael. Lift your leg up. Come on, now. Just a few more steps. That's it," she encouraged, all the while holding on to him tightly, feeling the masculine strength of him, hard and steady, pressing against her. "That's it, Michael. I'm going to guide you into the bathroom. I've already run a warm bath for you. My uncle Jimmy will help you in. The warm water will warm you up and then you can sleep.

"Do you think you can make it the rest of the way?" she asked with a worried frown. He was leaning even more heavily on her, as if his legs were getting harder and harder to move.

"Yeah," he muttered, trying to take a deep breath. "I…think I can manage.…" Determined, his eyes fluttered open and he struggled to keep them open. The light still hurt his eyes, but he could at least see a bit more of her. She was small and delicate, fragile, he thought immediately, and smelled…wonderful. Like vanilla, he decided. Just like vanilla and just as enticing.

His chin just grazed the top of her hair; a silky, soft cap of ebony curls that framed a face that could have been painted by one of the Masters, and cascaded down past her shoulders. His fingers itched to touch the curling strands to see if they were as soft as they looked. He wanted to twine his fingers through the silky strands and just let them slide lazily through his fingers.

"Are you an angel?" he asked with a crooked smile, staring down into her eyes.

Angela felt her stomach flip at the masculine intensity and interest in his gaze. Knowing she never could and never would allow that interest to amount to anything, she merely chuckled.

"Hardly, but my name *is* Angela."

"Told ya." Out of breath and strength, Michael had to pause at the top of the stairs to take a few deep breaths. His lungs must be thawing, he thought, since it didn't hurt nearly as much to breathe now. He realized her scent was something a bit stronger and sweeter than vanilla, but just as tantalizing.

"You *are* an angel," he whispered with a crooked grin. "My guardian angel," he said, leaning down and surprising them both by brushing his lips gently across hers in the lightest whisper of a kiss.

Angela's eyes widened and her stomach nosedived. For an instant, it felt as if someone had quickly tilted the floor from under her, nearly causing her to lose all balance. Astonished, she would have stepped back, but she couldn't because he was leaning on her, holding on to her tightly for balance.

His lips were soft and as sensuous and gentle as she'd expected. For an instant, just an instant, she lifted a hand to the front of his flannel shirt, telling herself she was gently going to push him away. But she found her fingers curling in the soft material as she allowed the kiss to continue.

Blinking in surprise at his own actions, Michael drew back, never moving his gaze from Angela's, his eyes confused and dazed, and not entirely from his accident.

He'd been right; she *was* his angel.

So why on earth did that thought scare the daylights out of him?

Chapter Two

Someone was in his room.

The next morning, Michael had just finished showering and shaving in the adjoining bath when he heard the footsteps. Draping a towel around his neck, he stepped into his jeans—which someone had thoughtfully washed and dried and left folded on a chair in the small, cozily decorated guest room. Then he slowly and quietly cracked open the adjoining door to the bedroom.

His entire body relaxed and he grinned at his pint-size intruder.

She couldn't be more than five or six, he figured, and almost a spitting miniature image of the beautiful angel he vaguely remembered from last night. Except she had perfectly round, thick-lensed glasses that framed her eyes, magnifying them so she looked a bit like a startled owl—

and a cowlick sticking up smack dab in the back of the middle of her head. She reminded him a bedraggled Raggedy Ann doll with those enormous blue eyes, rosy cheeks and cute button nose dotted all over with freckles. If ever he'd seen a kid born to look mischievous, this one was it, he thought in amusement.

"Hi," he said, opening the bathroom door wider and making her screech and nearly jump out of her shiny black shoes.

"You scared me," she accused, whirling to face him as he stepped into the room. "I thought you was sleeping."

He grinned, drying his still-damp face with the towel. "I *was* sleeping but now I'm not, and I'm sorry I scared you."

"I'm Emma," his pint-size visitor announced, crossing her arms across her chest and giving him a good long study. "Who are you?"

"Michael." He grinned and extended his hand to shake her little one. Pleased, she took it, then grinned and looked up at him curiously.

"You're big," she said, tilting her head back and squinting up at him from behind her glasses. "*Real* big." She rolled her big blue eyes for emphasis, then frowned.

"You got an owie on your forehead," she said, pointing to the bandage right between his eyes. Absently, he touched it; although he was sore and stiff, he was grateful the deep throbbing pain from last night had quieted to a dull roar.

"Does it hurt? I gots an owie on my knee, too. See?" Emma bent and pointed to her knee. "I fell down at school. It was bleeding and yucky." She straightened and began to nibble on her fingernail. "I'm in kindergarten and next year I'll be in first grade and then Mama says I'll go to school all day but I don't want to go all day 'cuz I'll miss mama and Uncle Jimmy and Mackenzie and Mahoney. They're my dogs and my bestest friends in the whole world. Where are you from? Mama says I'm not 'sposed to bother you. Am I bothering you?"

Amazed, Michael shook his head and grinned. He'd always had a soft spot for kids, and this one was a pistol. "Take a breath, kid," he said with a laugh. "You're making me dizzy, here."

"How come?" she asked with a frown.

With a chuckle, Michael shook his head again. He'd had no problem keeping up with the vicious minds of drug dealers, but keeping up with the maze of this inquisitive child's mind just might do him in. "How come…*what?*" he asked with a laugh.

"How come you're dizzy?" She screwed her face into a frown, walking around the room and skimming her hand atop the surface of everything she passed.

The guest room was utterly charming Michael had already decided after a quick but thorough inspection upon waking. Cozy, comfortable and filled with beautiful cherry antiques that had been lovingly refinished to their original splendor.

A four-poster Queen Anne bed gleamed in the morning sunlight. A beautiful antique chifforobe that had been refinished to its original patina covered almost an entire wall. A small, cherry English writing desk was tucked into one corner; atop the desk was a Waterford Depression-era vase filled with a bouquet of colorful dried flowers.

Everything fit, he realized, including the small-print blue wallpaper and the matching cotton curtains at the window, which afforded a perfect, cozy view of the snow-covered, icy world outside.

"Are you dizzy 'cuz of your owie?" Emma asked, turning to peer at him with an intensity that made Michael laugh.

"No, from so many questions," he said, reaching out to ruffle her hair.

"What's your name again?"

"Michael."

"Do you got any kids?"

"Nope, no kids. No dogs, either," he added trying to anticipate her next barrage of questions.

"How come?" Twin brows drew together worriedly. "Don't you like kids?"

He laughed, reaching for his flannel shirt off the bed. "Actually I love kids."

Her skinny shoulders moved up and down in a confused shrug. "Then how come you don't got none?"

Absently, Michael slipped his arms into his shirt, trying to think of an answer a six-year-old could understand. He wasn't about to explain that when his father was killed in the line of duty, leaving him and his brothers and sister fatherless and his mother a widow, he'd been devastated—they'd all been. But as the eldest son, he'd taken his father's death much harder than his brothers had and had always felt more of a sense of responsibility.

He knew when he became a cop that he could never do that to someone he loved—never expose her to or put her through such grief. Catching it in the line of duty was a daily fact of life for a city cop, especially for an undercover cop, so it just seemed easier to keep his life simple and his status single.

He brightened suddenly, buttoning his shirt. "Well, I

don't have a wife yet, and you need a wife before you can have kids because kids need a mother."

"Mama was a wife once. That's how she got to be my mother. But she's not a wife now." Emma's eyes widened suddenly. "But she could be a wife again," she said hopefully. "And a mother. I could ask her if she wants to be your wife—"

Slightly panicked, Michael wondered how to stop this runaway freight train. He lifted his hands in the air to try to head her off. "No, Emma, wait, I don't think—"

"No, really. I could ask her." Eyes bright, she stepped closer to him with a hopeful grin. "I don't think she'd mind. Then, if she was your wife, she could be a mother again and you could have kids." Emma leaned back on her heels. "You said you liked kids and I'm a kid—"

"So you claim," Michael said, trying not to laugh as he rolled up the sleeves of his shirt.

"But I am," Emma said fiercely, putting her hands on her hips. Her lower lip poked out defiantly and she held up six fingers. "I'm almost six, that makes me a kid."

"Six going on sixty," Michael grumbled in amusement.

"Where you from?" Emma asked, her mind jumping to another subject and making Michael heave a sigh of relief.

"Chicago." Amused, he pushed a hand through his still damp hair. "I'm from Chicago. I'm on vacation."

"I know where that's at. Mama says it's far away. But next summer, when I get out of school, Mama says maybe we're gonna take a train and go to Chicago to go shopping. It's gonna to take hours and hours," she added with a dramatic roll of her eyes. "Do you go to school?"

"Not anymore," Michael admitted, slipping his hands into the pockets of his jeans.

"Then what do you do?" she asked with a frown. "I mean, if you don't have a wife or kids, and don't go to school, what do you do?"

Explaining to a six-year-old that he was an undercover cop seemed far too complicated, besides, he was supposed to be keeping a low profile.

The last thing he wanted to do was risk having anyone find out *who* he was. Or worse, *where* he was.

So instead, he flashed her a smile and hedged. "My family owns an Irish deli," he said, going with the cover story he'd been using for two years. At least the part about his family owning an Irish deli was true. He wasn't about to start lying to a child.

"What's a deli?" she asked with a frown.

"It's kind of like a restaurant where we make sandwiches for people to eat."

"So you make sandwiches?" He nodded and she barreled on. "What kind of sandwiches? Peanut butter and jelly is my favorite. But sometimes I like peanut butter and chocolate. Do you got any brothers or sisters?"

Michael chuckled, realizing he was getting used to her machine-gun questioning. "Yep. I have five brothers and one sister."

"Really?" she breathed, her eyes widened in awe. "You got five brothers?" Taking a step closer to him, she frowned for a moment. "Barbie Myers says boys are yucky, but I'm not sure 'cuz I don't know any boys 'cept at school and I don't talk to them." She paused to swipe her fist across her nose. "But I'd love to have a sister. I don't got any brothers or a sister." Her solemn face brightened considerably, making him nervous. "But maybe if my mama got another husband and became a wife again, I could have a brother or a sister." Her grin was pure feminine wile. "Or maybe a brother *and* a sister?"

Uh-oh, she was back to that again, Michael thought and then grinned.

"What's this?" she asked, pointing to his laptop. Someone had put his duffel bag on the floor and his laptop, as well as all his notes, atop the small cherry writing desk.

"It's a computer."

Emma frowned. "Mama's got a computer downstairs, but I can't touch it 'cuz it's for business. We got a computer at school, too, but it's lots bigger and sometimes we get to draw pictures on it or write stories on it. I like to write stories best."

"So do I," Michael said, making her glance up at him in surprise.

"You do? What kind of stories?" She twirled one of her pigtails around a finger as she walked around the desk, eyeing the computer curiously. He could almost see the wheels of her mind churning.

"Mysteries. I like to write mysteries." It was true, he thought. At least, that's what he'd been planning and dreaming about for the past ten years. Now whether he could do it or not was another…story, so to speak.

"You mean scary stories," she clarified. She frowned but then brightened suddenly. "I like to write funny stories about my dogs, Mahoney and Mackenzie. They like peanut butter and jelly, too. And M&M's. We all like M&Ms. Do you think we could write stories together sometime?" She glanced up at him hopefully.

"Sure," Michael said. "I'll even show you how to use my computer."

Her eyes went wide as saucers and she took a step closer to him, lifting her face up to his. "Really?" she said.

"Really," Michael confirmed.

"Emma Marie DiRosa."

Emma froze. "Uh-oh," she whispered, her gaze darting from Michael to the open doorway where her mother stood, arms crossed across her chest, a look of mild displeasure on her face. The urchin's cheeks paled and she whirled.

"Hi, Mama," Emma said brightly, skipping toward her mother and trying to ignore the warning signs of trouble in her mother's eyes. "This is Michael. And I'm not bothering him, honest."

"Mmm, yes, I can see that you're not bothering him," Angela said in amusement, leaning against the doorjamb and glancing at Michael as she pushed her hair from her face.

He looked none the worse for wear this morning, she decided. But even without his stubby growth of beard, he still had that dangerous masculine look about him, that male intensity that had her pulse kicking up and her heart scrambling.

When his gaze locked on hers, Angela shifted nervously in the doorway. This morning, she could see his eyes were green. They were huge, clear and deep eyes, with an intensity that made a woman feel as if she were the only thing in the world—at least his world. It was totally unnerving, she decided, annoyed.

It had been years since she'd been so aware of a man's presence, years since her body had felt something—*any-thing*—merely because of being in the same room with a man.

Absently, she rubbed a hand up and down her arm, feeling as if her skin were tingling, which was ridiculous, just as ridiculous as her response to him last night.

She hadn't been able to sleep after he'd kissed her. Her

body had hummed and sang for a good long time, keeping her awake. She tossed and turned, wondering, just…wondering. It was foolishness, she knew.

He was a stranger and would no doubt be on his way to his destination soon. No sense wondering or fantasizing about a stranger who probably had a life and a wife back in the real world where he came from.

Instinctively, Angela's gaze settled on his hands, and she noted he wore no jewelry of any kind. No wedding ring, which meant nothing, she told herself. A lot of married men didn't wear wedding rings. Then again, last night he'd said he didn't need anyone called, and if he was married, he certainly would have wanted his wife—if he had one—notified of his accident.

Realizing that she was simply still staring at him, Angela dragged her gaze away from him and scolded herself for allowing her imagination to run away with her over one harmless kiss that he probably didn't even remember this morning.

Harmless foolishness, she told herself again and turned her attention to her daughter. But she was vividly aware that he was still just standing there, big as life, watching her.

"Mama?" Emma grinned and tugged on her mother's hand to get her attention. "Guess what?"

"The Cubs are going to win the pennant?"

Emma giggled. "Mama! You always say that when I say, 'Guess what.'"

"That's because that's my best guess."

Beaming, Emma swung her mom's hand to and fro. "Michael's on vacation."

"Mmm, yes I know," Angela said with a smile, glancing at Michael, surprised to find both amusement and amazement in his eyes.

"And did you know that he doesn't go to school anymore, but he makes sandwiches for people, and he has five brothers and one sister—" Emma paused to hold up five fingers so the exact number would be perfectly clear "—Five brothers and I don't got none," she added in complaint again. "He lives far away in Chicago and he doesn't got any kids 'cuz he doesn't have a wife, and—"

"And you found all this out because you were *not* bothering him, right?" Angela said with a grin, reaching down to tighten and straighten one of her daughter's pigtails before giving her an affectionate pat.

"Right." Emma grinned. "And he likes kids, too, Mama."

"Well, it's early in the day yet, Em. Give him time and he could change his mind," she said, exchanging an amused look with Michael.

"And Michael writes stories just like me." Emma turned to beam at him. "He's got a computer and everything. See?" She pointed to Michael's laptop. "But he writes scary mystery stories, right?" Emma asked, and Michael nodded in confirmation. "And he said that sometime he would show me how to use his computer and then we could write stories together, right?" Emma said, glancing at Michael, who nodded.

Not certain if her daughter was telling tall tales, Angela frowned. It was only in the past year, since Em had started school, that she'd begun to worry about the lack of a father figure in her daughter's life. Going to school had given Em her first taste of being "different," of not having a father. Angela's ex-husband had never bothered to even see his daughter.

Her uncle Jimmy had tried to fill in as best as he could, but since his last heart attack, he didn't have the stamina or the physical ability that a younger man would have, making it difficult for him to be the kind of father figure he'd wanted to be.

But that didn't mean she wanted her daughter approaching strangers for companionship or company. The fact that her daughter felt the loss enough to do so not only worried her, but saddened her. It couldn't be helped, she'd told herself on more than one occasion. Having no father was better than one who couldn't tell the truth—about anything.

"Emma, I'm not certain—"

"I did tell her I'd teach her how to use my computer," Michael confirmed with a grin for both of them, hoping to defuse some of the suspicion in Angela's eyes. Interesting how those blue eyes of hers shadowed and darkened when she was suspicious.

What, he wondered, was she so suspicious of?

"And I also told her we could write stories together some time," he added with a lift of his brow, waiting for her to challenge him.

"That's really very kind of you, but certainly not necessary," Angela hedged, feeling both grateful for his kindness toward her precocious daughter, as well as embarrassment at her daughter for apparently putting him on the spot.

Michael shrugged, never taking his gaze from Angela's. "I know. But I'd like to. I made the offer," he specified, so there wouldn't be any misunderstanding. "I think it's great that Emma's got such a vivid imagination."

"Easy for you to say," Angela said with a roll of her eyes, mimicking her daughter and making Michael laugh.

"Wait, Mama, there's more," Emma barreled on.

"Charming," Angela said nervously. "I can hardly wait." She forced a smile and looked at her daughter, trying to brace herself for whatever was to come. "All right, go on, sweetheart."

Emma beamed at her mother. "Michael doesn't got any kids 'cuz he doesn't got a wife, so I told him maybe *you* could be his wife, and then he could have some kids and I could have a brother or a sister, or maybe a brother *and* a sister." Her daughter's eyes shone with hope. "What do you think?"

"You…you…" Stunned, Angela's embarrassed gaze darted from her daughter to Michael, who stood there trying not to grin. Angela let her eyes slide closed for a moment to try to get a handle on her embarrassment. "Em, you asked Michael if he wanted me for his *wife?*" she all but croaked, and Emma nodded enthusiastically.

"Isn't it a good idea?" her daughter asked with a happy, toothless smile, making Angela all but groan.

"Oh, it's…just…terrific," Angela muttered miserably, looking everywhere—anywhere—but at Michael. "Sweetheart," she began slowly, taking her daughter by the shoulders if only to get her to stand still for one moment. "Do you remember what we talked about last month?" She cast a quick glance at Michael. "When you asked Mr. Parsons if he wanted me to be his wife?" Eighty-three-year-old cranky, cantankerous Mr. Parsons.

Brows drawn together, Emma nodded slowly. "Yeah, but Mama, this is different. Mr. Parsons is old, *real* old," she added with a roll of her eyes for emphasis, "and sometimes he's grumpy." Emma shrugged her shoulders. "Michael's old, too, but he's not grumpy," she finished, satisfied she'd made her case. "Who wants an old and grumpy husband to have babies with?" she asked, making Angela close her eyes and silently pray for patience.

Or for the floor to open up and swallow her. Either would be welcome at the moment.

"Emma," Angela began again, trying not to blush, but one look at Michael's amused face told her she'd lost the battle. "I think," she began slowly, mortified, "I think it's time for you to do your morning chores."

"But Mama—"

"Scoot," Angela said, giving her daughter an affectionate pat on the backside. "The dogs need to be fed and let out, and the breakfast table needs to be set."

"But—"

"But nothing," Angela said, pointing her finger down the hall. "Go do your chores. No chores, no making chocolate chip cookies this afternoon."

"Drats!" Crestfallen, Emma shot a conspiratorial look at Michael over her shoulder as she glumly marched out the door. When he winked at her daughter and made her smile, Angela pretended not to see it, pretended not to be charmed.

"I'm so sorry," Angela said with a shake of her head. "She knows better than to bother our guests." Feeling the need to explain, Angela shook her head. "She's been on this kick for a couple of months about having a brother or sister. But I never thought she'd resort to trying to peddle me off to strangers." Then, realizing what she'd said and what her daughter had done, she couldn't help but laugh.

"Even really *old* strangers like me?" Michael asked with an amused lift of his brow.

"I really am sorry. I hope she didn't put you on the spot or make you uncomfortable."

"Nah, don't worry about it," he said, a wicked gleam in his eyes. "We hadn't even gotten to the negotiation part."

"Negotiation part?" Angela repeated, stunned. Then realizing he was smiling, she relaxed. "I get it, that's a joke. Isn't it?" she asked hopefully, making him laugh. Although she felt foolish, Angela was grateful he had a sense of humor. "Michael, look, I really am sorry."

"Not a problem," Michael said, wondering exactly who Mr. Parsons was and what his relationship was with the woman he considered *his* angel. If he didn't know better, he'd swear he was feeling a bout of jealousy, which was ridiculous, since he didn't even know this woman.

Anxious to change the subject, Angela looked at him, wanting to get back to business. "How are you feeling this morning?"

"Not too bad." He rubbed the back of his head. "My head's settled down to a dull roar but I think I'll make it. I can't thank you enough for what you did for me last night," Michael said. "I drove up from Chicago, and I was so exhausted and so lost in thought, I didn't even realize I'd driven right into the mouth of the storm until it was too late." He shrugged. "I'm not usually so scatterbrained, but it was the first day of my first vacation in two years."

"I understand," she said with a nod. "And I'm glad you were able to find your way here. Chester's a small town. There isn't another inn or motel for about twelve miles." She hesitated. "I hope you don't mind, but I called Andy's Garage in town to tell them about your car. You said you had the accident right after the exit off the interstate?" He nodded as she glanced toward the window. "We had about thirty inches of snow and the weatherman is predicting another eight to ten inches more by tomorrow night. So it's going to be a couple of days before the plows can even dig us out. All the roads are closed and Andy said he can't even go get your car and tow it into his shop until the roads are cleared. So I'm afraid you're going to be stuck here for a few days."

Michael shrugged and then glanced around, suddenly pleased by the thought of staying here for a few more days. He'd wanted somewhere isolated, where he'd have peace and quiet and be away from the prying eyes of the press. This place, isolated and now buried in snow, seemed perfect. If he couldn't get out, certainly no one else could get in, giving him even more privacy and security.

He glanced at Angela and felt something strange spark to life inside. She was one helluva good-looking woman, certainly not a hardship to spend more time with. Besides, he had a feeling it was going to be very interesting getting to know her and her daughter.

Emma was an adorable kid, with a mind as curious as he'd ever encountered. He had a feeling she was a pistol to parent. His mother had had seven children, but he had a feeling the little pint-size walking questionnaire was more of a handful than he and all of his brothers and sister put together.

His admiration for Emma's mother—her apparently *single* mother—went up several notches.

He found his gaze drawn to Angela, liking what he saw. She didn't wear a hint of makeup that he could see and, in spite of having a child, her figure, clad in jeans and a turtleneck, was more of a teenager's than a mother. Not that she didn't have curves in all the right places. Sweet, womanly curves that would draw a man's eye and his attention.

Yet it wasn't just her beauty, but something else about her that pulled at him in a way a woman hadn't in a long time. Something he didn't quite understand yet, or couldn't quite explain. Perhaps it should have frightened him, but at the moment, it didn't.

"Like I said, I'm on vacation for the next month, and I've got no set plans or destination, so I'm in no rush. In fact, if you've got the room, I'd just as soon stay here for the month." It had been a spur-of-the-moment decision; something about her and the pint-size urchin was pulling at him, but he preferred to ignore it, and instead focus on the peace and serenity he felt here—the quiet calm after the turmoil of the city and the job of the past two years.

Michael glanced around the room, pleased. "This seems like the perfect place to get some writing done. It's quiet, peaceful and secluded enough that I don't have to worry about many interruptions."

The thought of him staying for a whole month made Angela's nerves jangle, but she tried very hard to hide it with a bright smile. "Well, you're more than welcome. And I promise I'll try to keep Emma out of your hair," she said with a smile and a sigh. "Emma means well, but she's just a bit precocious and tends to rattle on like a freight train."

"I think she's fabulous," Michael said, meaning it. "You're very lucky. My sister's expecting twins in the spring and, to be honest, I can't wait."

Cocking her head, she looked at him and he saw the suspicion and the wariness in her eyes again. For some reason, it fascinated and annoyed him.

"You really do have five brothers and a sister?" she asked.

She was definitely skittish, he realized. About men? Or just about him? He wasn't quite sure. But how on earth could this woman think he'd lie to a kid?

He didn't know, but the mere thought that she did made him sad and just a tad offended.

"Do you really think I'd lie to a child?" he asked carefully, wondering who on earth had lied to her or to her child to make her so suspicious of men.

She had the good grace to blush again, gently shifting her gaze from his and licking her lips. Michael watched her and felt an uncommon tightening in his gut as his gaze followed the tip of her tongue.

Her mouth was full, soft and very sensual, he remembered, but couldn't remember *why* he remembered it.

Had he kissed her? he wondered.

Rubbing the back of his neck, Michael frowned, trying to remember exactly what had happened last night. His memories were all fuzzy, but somehow he remembered kissing her.

And he knew he'd enjoyed it.

"I'm sorry," Angela said, glancing down at the floor and shifting uncomfortably before bringing her gaze back to his. "I didn't mean to imply you'd lied to Emma, it's just—"

"Yes, you did," Michael said softly. "I really do have five brothers and one sister," he told her with an easy smile. "I'm the oldest boy, I've got five younger brothers and one sister. Maggy's the oldest of us all and the only girl."

"Poor thing," Angela said in sympathy, making him grin.

"She's felt that way many a time, I'm sure," Michael admitted. "I also have an interfering, meddling, matchmaking seventy-two-year-old grandfather who could give little Emma a run for her money both in deed and word. I'm really from Chicago, born and raised there, and my family owns an Irish deli on the South Side of Chicago, Gallagher's Irish Deli—it's been in my family for three generations."

"So, Michael Gallagher," she said, trying out his full name and realizing it fit him. "You're really a writer?" Angela asked with a lift of her brow and glancing at his laptop on the table.

He laughed. "Well, let's say I'm trying to be."

"I don't think I've ever met a writer before. I think that's fascinating."

He shrugged. "Yeah, well, don't get too excited. I guess you could say this month-long vacation is make-or-break time for me. I'm finally taking the time I need to just sit down and write." He shrugged again. "We'll see what happens. If I'm any good, maybe I'll give up my day job," he said with a laugh and a shrug. "We'll see."

Seemingly satisfied, she nodded. "Well, like I said, you're welcome to stay. We're closed until the first week in December when we open for the annual Chester Lake Christmas Festival." She smiled at the confusion on his face. "It's a huge annual festival we're known for. People drive up here from all over to attend. You're more than welcome to stay here until your car's ready, or until you're ready to leave, whichever comes first. I think it's probably a good idea for you to rest for a few days before you start driving again, anyway."

He nodded, pleased. "I appreciate it."

"I own the inn along with my uncle Jimmy." She grinned. "You haven't met him yet. He's a bit grumpy, but a kinder heart you'll never find. And he plays a mean game of checkers, not to mention cards, and is not above cheating, so don't let him con you," she warned with a shake of her finger.

"I'll try to remember that." He grinned. "But I've got years of experience with my grandfather, who's a con man personified," Michael added with a laugh, feeling a rush of overwhelming love for his family.

Then a thought had him frowning. "Do you and your uncle run the inn alone?"

"Yep, it's just us," Angela sighed. "During the summer or the busy Christmas season, I usually hire some kids from town to help out. Other than that, we tend to get by with just us." Angela glanced at her watch. "Things at the inn will be a lot less regimented than normal, but breakfast should be ready in about thirty minutes if you're interested."

"Actually, I'm starving," Michael said, rubbing his stomach. He realized he hadn't eaten since he'd grabbed a doughnut on his way out of the city yesterday.

"Lunch is generally just sandwiches or homemade soup. Dinner is usually around six, depending on what time I get finished with my daily chores."

"Sounds good."

Angela glanced out the window again so she wouldn't have to look directly at him. It just made her far too aware of him, and difficult to keep her mind on what she was saying, thinking. "I'm planning on making lasagna tonight. I hope you like it."

"Homemade lasagna?" he asked so hopefully that she laughed.

"Definitely. From scratch. I know it may be old-fashioned, but I make everything from scratch. No TV dinners, no microwave meals, no canned soup for my family or my guests."

"I think I've died and gone to heaven," Michael said with a roll of his eyes. "I'm lucky if I can boil water, so anytime I can get a homecooked meal I'm in hog heaven."

"Well, consider yourself in heaven, then," she said. "Thirty minutes?"

He nodded. "I'll see you downstairs."

"Just follow your nose to the kitchen," she instructed before quietly closing his door behind her and heading down the hall, wondering what on earth was wrong with her.

She'd actually been flirting with a guest! A guest her own daughter had tried to pawn her off on. Angela shook her head, not certain if she was more amused or annoyed.

And she wasn't much better than Emma, openly flirting with him like she was young and carefree, which she most certainly was not. At twenty-six, she supposed some would still consider her young, but with the responsibility she'd had for the past six years, she'd stopped thinking of herself as young and carefree years ago.

She couldn't remember the last time she'd flirted with a man, especially a man like Michael. And she had a cardinal rule about not getting involved with any of their guests. It was not just bad business, but a very bad precedent to set.

Her guests were her lifeblood, necessary not just to her business but to her way of life, and she'd worked far too hard to do anything to jeopardize the security and tranquility she'd managed to provide for herself and her daughter.

Not to mention the fact that she wasn't in the least bit interested in getting involved with a man—no matter how gorgeous he was or how kind he was to her daughter.

All she had to do was look at her precious daughter to remember what her bad judgment and bad marriage had almost cost her. She'd blindly trusted another man once before, believing he'd never lie or deceive her. And he had, breaking her heart and forever changing her ability to trust.

Determined to stop being so foolish, Angela headed downstairs to start breakfast and to put her interest in and curiosity about her newest guest out of her mind.

Chapter Three

Feeling better—at least emotionally—than he had in a long time, Michael spent a very productive twenty minutes unpacking the meager clothing in his duffel bag, setting up his laptop and getting his notes into some semblance of order on the writing desk. With a whole month stretching endlessly before him, he couldn't wait to get started writing.

Finally, his empty growling stomach insisted he follow his nose. The scent of sizzling bacon drifted through the entire inn, and with an attack of hunger nipping at him, he decided to head downstairs.

When he reached the bottom step, he stopped abruptly in front of the two growling dogs who were perched protectively at the foot of the stairs and not particularly thrilled with the sight of him.

"Good boys," he muttered nervously, lifting a hand out

to try to pet them. His hand froze when they stepped closer, crowding his legs and baring their teeth while growling even louder.

"Good boys," Michael muttered again, glancing around to see if anyone was about to come rescue him. "Angela?" he called. "Emma?" He swallowed hard. "Help."

"So you met the mutts?" A male voice called, causing Michael to glance up and look across the room. A spry old man—about sixty, with a shock of gray hair and wearing a shirt in a style and color that was loud enough to possibly break the sound barrier, was limping toward him, leaning heavily on a cane. "Mackenzie! Mahoney!" the old man barked, snapping the tip of his cane sharply on the wood floor. "What the devil are you two idiots doing?" Glaring at the dogs, he snapped his cane on the floor again. "You know you're not supposed to scare the guests! It's bad for business." The old man used his cane to gently nudge the dogs out of the way. "Get in the kitchen," he ordered, pointing his cane at the dogs and making them hang their heads in shame. "And stop scaring the guests. You know better."

Letting out a relieved sigh, Michael patted his heart. "Thanks."

"No problem. I'm Jimmy, Angela's uncle." The old man held out his free hand while his other held on to his cane.

"Michael. Michael Gallagher." He took the old man's hand, noted it was rough and calloused, and shook it. "Thanks for taking me in last night."

"Damn fool night to be out driving if you ask me," Jimmy said with a huff. "And don't worry about the mutts. They may look fierce, but they're afraid of their own shadows." Jimmy grinned. "Kinda like me." He looked at Michael carefully. "You hungry?"

"Starved," Michael admitted with a grin.

"Come on, then. Let's grab some grub." Jimmy led the way, his cane clicking softly on the floor. "Play any cards?" Jimmy asked conversationally.

"A little," Michael admitted, trying not to grin and grateful Angela had forewarned him. "My grandfather and I used to play all the time when I was younger."

"You don't say?" Jimmy asked with a smile and a gleam in his eye. "What about checkers?"

Michael laughed, reaching around the man to push open the swinging door that led into what his nose told him was the kitchen. His eyes widened in pleasant surprise. The kitchen was long and wide, taking up almost the entire back of the inn. Decorated in the same New England blue, the counters were stainless steel and spotless, and the appliances were state-of-the-art, also stainless steel. There was a six-burner stove, a double oven that took up nearly a quarter of one wall, an array of appliances and what he assumed where cooking gadgets, as well as a long square Parsons table with seating for twelve dominating the middle of the room. Each of the twelve wooden ladder-backed chairs were covered in a delicate blue patterned cushion to match the blue print wallpaper and the blue-and-white dotted Swiss curtains at the window.

A huge, roaring fireplace took up one entire wall and cast soft light and welcoming heat into the room, giving it a small cozy feel in spite of its large size. In the corner, near what he assumed was the back door, stood the two dogs he'd encountered on his way downstairs. They sat on a blue rug, looking mournfully at the breakfast table.

"Play a mean game of checkers, as well," Michael admitted, sighing deeply in pleasure at the wonderful, aromatic smells drifting through the kitchen.

"Mama made pancakes, Michael," Emma said, glancing up at him with a grin. "She makes the best pancakes in the whole world." She pointed to the wooden chair next to her. "You can sit here." Emma grinned, patting the chair cushion. "Right between me and Mama."

Jimmy pulled out his own chair, his gaze still on Michael. "Maybe tonight you and me can have a friendly game of checkers, if you've got a mind too?" he asked casually, too casually for the gleam in his eyes, before leaning his cane against the table and plopping down in his chair.

"Maybe we can," Michael agreed, watching Angela, who was standing at the stove, flipping the last of the batch of pancakes she'd made.

Watching her work, watching the way those slender, delicate hands flipped pancakes and deftly turned bacon, all the while never losing track of the coffee that was brewing or the needs of the people at the table, he realized she wasn't just beautiful but also incredibly competent. That was something he'd always admired in a woman.

Smart, beautiful and competent. It could be, he knew, quite a heady combination if a man wasn't careful. But he'd always been a careful man, ever since his father's death when he'd made his life's choices and resolutions.

He'd made the choice willingly, he reminded himself, certain the life of a cop was exactly what he'd always wanted, what he'd been born to be. But right now, sitting in this cozy kitchen, all but snowed in, with the warmth of a fireplace behind him and the warmth of a family surrounding him, he felt a pang of loneliness and longing so deep that it shocked him.

He glanced at Emma and wondered for the first time

what it would be like to have his own child. He'd always adored children and he couldn't imagine never holding his very own in his arms—and in his heart.

His gaze shifted to Angela, who had lifted the platter of pancakes and was now expertly juggling the coffeepot and the platter as she made her way to the table.

A wife, he thought, watching her. What would it be like to have a home like this? A family like this?

A wife like her?

Michael shook the thought away. He didn't know because he'd simply never considered it as a possibility—which it wasn't, he reminded himself.

Perhaps, he mused, that was the cause for the vague disillusionment and dissatisfaction he'd been feeling the past few years. Maybe it was that he'd made a decision without seriously considering all the ramifications. The feelings of emptiness that had been simmering inside for the past few years seemed to linger, crowding his belly and crawling through his mind.

He'd made his choice, he thought firmly, and at the time, he was absolutely certain it had been the best choice, the right choice.

The only choice.

But had he made the right choice?

Michael glanced at Emma and then at Angela, sighing deeply and feeling a peculiar, lingering loneliness. He didn't know, and for the first time in his life, the thought that he might not have, scared him.

After breakfast, Angela decided the best cure for her own case of anxiety and nerves was simply to ignore her new guest and to settle down into her normal, daily routine.

Guests or not, there were chores to do, laundry to be sorted and washed, meals to be prepared and, this morning, the driveway to snowplow and additional firewood to cut.

Normally, the inn had firewood delivered from town, but since the roads were closed and they were running low on firewood, she knew there'd be no deliveries, at least not today or tomorrow. And since deliveries were only done during the work week, she knew that if they got the additional snow the weatherman was predicting, they just might run out of firewood before Monday morning—if Grady at the lumberyard could even get his trucks through by then. And she knew better than to take a chance. If they lost power, it could be out for days; the large fireplaces in the kitchen and living room would be the only source of heat and light, making firewood not a luxury, but a definite necessity.

After shooing everyone out of her kitchen—she'd settled Emma in the living room with one of her favorite coloring books and a stack of crayons—Angela cleaned up the kitchen, loaded the dishwasher and then mopped up the floor. She could get a few loads in the wash while she also started her spaghetti sauce for dinner.

As she headed upstairs toward Emma's room, she could hear quiet murmurs coming from Michael's room. She didn't remember seeing Emma in the living room when she passed through and, on a hunch, with her arms full of dirty laundry, she paused at the partially open doorway leading into Michael's room.

Emma was seated at the little writing desk, Michael's laptop open and on the writing surface in front of her. He was kneeling beside her, patiently explaining the intricacies of the computer to her daughter. Something about seeing them, heads bent together, touched and warmed

Angela's heart. She stood there quietly for a moment, watching the large man with the big hands patiently instruct and guide her daughter.

He'd make a wonderful father, she thought absently, wondering again why the man wasn't married.

"See, this is the button that saves everything," Michael patiently explained, pointing to the keyboard. "You push it just like this, Em, and once you push it, then everything you've written, your whole story, will be saved inside the computer."

"Like this?" After pushing the button, Emma lifted her face to his, a hopeful smile on her face.

"That's exactly right, Em." Michael ruffled her hair affectionately. "Now, when you go back to write some more, all you have to do is open the box that says: Emma's Story, and everything you wrote will be right there."

"Cool." Wide-eyed and pleased, Emma stared at the computer screen. "This is fun," she announced with a grin, turning to look up at him adoringly. "You teach good."

He laughed. "Well, you learn good, too, pint-size." He ruffled her hair again. "And you learn very quickly."

Her daughter was so eager to please, Angela thought with a sigh, shifting her load of clothes. She'd thought for certain she'd been giving and providing her daughter with everything she wanted and needed to grow up happy, safe and secure. But seeing her now with Michael, seeing the longing in her daughter's eyes, Angela wasn't so sure. The thought of her daughter being unhappy for even a moment was completely unsettling.

She'd been trying to provide Emma with everything a child needed—everything but the one thing her daughter wanted and perhaps needed most—a father.

And until this morning, until she saw the deep longing in her daughter's eyes when she looked at Michael, Angela had never realized just how much Emma might have missed having a father in her life.

Backing away from the doorway before she could be seen, Angela shifted her load of dirty laundry to her other arm and then headed downstairs, trying not to berate herself. But she simply couldn't get around the guilt, or the fact that if she'd chosen a husband more carefully—if she'd been wiser and more mature, and considered the fact that the man she'd chosen to spend her life with wouldn't just be her husband, but a father to her unborn children, as well—perhaps, just perhaps, she would have been more cautious.

"Poor choices lead to poor consequences," her grandmother used to say. And she was living proof of the old adage, she thought as she loaded darks into the washing machine, scooped in some laundry detergent, closed the lid and started the machine. She'd made her decisions, right or wrong, and now both she and Emma had to live with the consequences because Angela knew that as much as Emma wanted or needed a father, there was no getting around the fact that *she* could never give a man that kind of trust again. Not ever, no matter how kind or patient he was with her daughter.

With the first four loads of laundry washed, folded and lined up in the laundry room waiting to be carried upstairs and put away, and with her spaghetti sauce for her lasagna tonight simmering on the stove, Angela decided it was time to tackle the wood.

She was just slipping on her heavy down coat when Michael sauntered into the kitchen.

He frowned as she wrapped a heavy woolen scarf around her neck. "I thought you said the roads were closed."

"They are," she said, pulling her worn leather work gloves out of her coat pockets and pulling one on.

"Then where are you going?" he asked.

"To chop some wood."

"You're going outside to chop wood?"

She nodded, busying herself with tugging on her winter boots, unaware that he was staring at her as if she'd just announced she intended to give birth—right there on the kitchen floor. "It's Wednesday, the roads won't even be clean or cleared until Friday at the earliest, and if we get that additional snow they're predicting, the delivery truck won't be able to get through until the first of next week at the earliest. We need wood for the fireplaces before then." She zipped her boots up, then stood and looked at him. "So I'm going to go outside and chop some."

"You? Alone?" The tone of his voice had her back going up and she narrowed her gaze on him.

"Yes, me alone." She tugged on her other glove a bit harder than necessary and then glanced up at him. She didn't particularly care for his tone of voice. It implied he didn't think her capable of chopping wood. Determined to be pleasant since he was a guest, she managed a smile. "Do you have a problem with that?"

Uh-oh. He was no dummy. He knew when he'd stuck his foot in his mouth, and apparently he just had.

"No, not a problem," he hedged and then smiled. Her face didn't change or soften, he noted, realizing he'd probably unintentionally insulted her. "But if you give me a minute, I'll get my jacket and help."

Angela stiffened, her discomfort clear. "Excuse me, Michael, but I don't need your help. I've been chopping wood for years. Nothing to it when you've got a good, sharp ax and a strong back. I've got both." She hesitated, annoyed at having him treat her like some frail, fragile female. She'd been taking care of herself and her daughter far too long to be either frail or fragile; and as for the female part, well, there wasn't much she could do about that. She managed a smile, but it cost her. "Besides, you're a guest, Michael. Guests don't do chores or maintenance. It's not something we require here at the inn."

"Oh, I see," he said, leaning his hands on the back of one of the wooden ladder chairs and studying her. "So then when you took me in last night and gave me medical attention, was that part of the usual hospitality of the inn?"

"Well, no, of course not," she said, a bit confused. "Most of our guests don't require medical attention. It was special circumstances."

"Mmm, yes, I understand that," he said with a nod as he reached into his pants pocket and pulled out his wallet. He was grateful his badge was still tucked in his second wallet in his glove box, where he always kept it when he was undercover. "So, how much do I owe you then?" He glanced up at her just in time to see her eyes cloud and her frown. "For the medical attention?"

She laughed to cover the sudden insult she felt. "Don't be ridiculous," she said stiffly, slipping her clenched fists into her coat pockets. "I'm certainly not going to charge you for helping to take care of you last night. You had a car accident, Michael. It's not like I'd just leave you wounded and bleeding."

"I see," he said carefully. "So what you're saying basically is that I needed help and since you were able and capable of providing that help and did, for me to reject it or offer to pay for it would be an insult?"

"Yes," she said, grateful that he finally understood. She continued to stare at him for a moment, not liking the light that suddenly lit his eyes. He was definitely up to something, she realized. What, she wasn't sure.

"Well, Angela, since I needed help and you willingly provided that help last night, I don't see why I can't do the same. Return the favor so to speak?" He grinned at her, a grin that only annoyed her further since she realized he'd just quickly and neatly bushwhacked her. "I've got a very strong back, and as long as you provide the ax, I don't see why you won't let me help you out by chopping some wood for you. We can simply call it returning a favor."

"Returning a favor?" she repeated dubiously with a lift of her brow.

"You can also consider it saving my hide if you want." His fingers relaxed on the back of the chair and he smiled. "You see, old as my grandfather is, if he ever found out one of his able-bodied grandsons sat around and did nothing while a woman went out and chopped wood in the snowy, freezing cold, well now, I guarantee my grandfather would box my ears in, and rightly so." Absently, Michael rubbed a hand over his jaw. "Politically correct or not, Angela, my brothers and I were brought up with an old-fashioned sense of manners and morals and, like it or not, I figure I'm far too old to change now."

"There's a name for men like you," she said softly, genuinely touched by his kindness and consideration and more impressed than she believed possible.

Here was a very rare man, a man who'd risk looking like

a fool and being ridiculed simply to stick to the values and beliefs he'd been brought up with. She was stunned; she'd forgotten men like him still existed. Something about him, about the way he was with her, with her daughter, had managed to touch her guarded heart. Perhaps that's why he made her so nervous.

"Yeah," he admitted with a sigh. "I know. I've probably been called all of them. Chauvinistic. Old-fashioned." He gave her a rather thin smile. "Pig." He shrugged. "I've probably heard them all, but feel free to fire away if it makes you feel better."

Smiling, she tugged off her gloves, slipped them in her pockets and then crossed the room to him. "Thoughtful," she said, meeting his gaze and refusing to draw her gaze away, even when it made her stomach dance. "Very thoughtful." She stood on tiptoe and brushed her lips against his cheek before backing away again.

Her scent, that wonderful heavenly scent, danced through the air, infiltrating his breathing space. He inhaled deeply, trying to capture it.

"Thank you, Michael. I truly appreciate your help."

"You're welcome." Michael touched his face, stunned to find his cheek was tingling and his stomach knotted from a simple kiss on the cheek. He watched as she pulled her coat off and hung it up on the coatrack by the back door. "Ax out back in one of those buildings?" he asked, pointing toward the window where some of the large white buildings behind the inn were visible.

"Right outside in that large white building to the right." She stood next to him, pointing as well, realizing just how much bigger he was than her. He made her feel small and feminine, something she hadn't felt in a long time. "That's the toolshed. I keep all the sharp tools hung up on a rack set up high so Emma can't get to them. It should be right next to the snowblower."

"Snowblower, huh?" Michael muttered still staring out the window.

She laughed. "Don't go getting any ideas, Michael. The wood will be fine."

As he went upstairs to get his coat and borrow some warm gloves from her uncle, Angela began pulling out the makings for her famous chocolate chip cookies. If the man was going to chop wood for her, the least she could do was make him some fresh coffee and homemade cookies.

In the end, Michael ended up chopping enough wood to get them through the entire weekend. Then he plowed the driveway with the snowblower, clearing a large path so that if and when the roads opened, Angela would be able to get out to do her shopping or chores.

It was nearly dark by the time Angela heard him finishing up the driveway. After brewing a fresh pot of hot coffee, Angela decided to take a cup out to him, along with several still-warm cookies that she and Emma had baked.

"You missed lunch," Angela said by way of greeting as Michael came out of the toolshed, pausing to close and lock the heavy wooden door behind him. She held out the hot cup of coffee to him, struggling to find her balance on the icy, slippery ground.

"My heroine," he said, eyeing the cup. He reached for it, blowing on it for a moment before drinking greedily. He was chilled through and through, but nothing near as bad as last night.

"I brought you some cookies, as well."

"Homemade?" he asked hopefully.

"Only kind allowed in my house," she said, extending the napkin with the cookies in them.

He bit into one, letting his eyes close in pleasure as he sighed. "This is the best cookie I've ever eaten."

"Well, dinner will be ready in about an hour, so don't ruin your appetite."

"Dinner?" One brow lifted. "I get dinner, too?" he asked hopefully, making her laugh. "If you keep feeding me like this, I may never leave," he said with a smile, sipping his coffee and popping another cookie whole into his mouth.

"Well, Michael," she said as they began walking together back toward the house. One foot almost slid out from under her, and he grabbed her arm to steady her. "If you keep doing all this work, I may have to put you to work."

Still holding on to her, he hesitated for a moment, looking at her. "You know, that's not a bad idea."

"What?" she asked.

"Putting me to work while I'm here. You said you usually hire help for the Christmas festival. It's less than a month away, right? Well, why hire someone when I'm right here."

She was thoughtful for a moment. "You mean, like have you help out in exchange for what…your room and board?"

"Sounds like a plan to me, what do you think?" Michael asked.

It sounded perfectly reasonable to her. And would save her cash during the time the inn was closed for the season. If all she had to provide was food, which she had to cook for her family anyway, as well as a place for him to stay, which was also available at no additional cost to her, it might give them more of a cash cushion for the off-season next year.

"Actually, Michael, I think it's a great idea, but I'll have to run it by Uncle Jimmy, see what he says. He does own half of the inn."

Michael shrugged, draining his coffee cup. "That's fine with me."

She nodded, pleased. "I'll talk to him—" Even though Michael still had one hand on her, her feet started to go out from under her and she gave a soft cry, struggling to maintain her balance.

Instinctively, Michael grabbed her with both hands, letting the coffee cup fall to the ground. "Whoa, whoa," he said, reaching for the lapels of her coat and all but lifting her off her feet to prevent her from falling. "Easy there."

Wanting to make sure he had a firm hold on her, he transferred his hands from her lapels to her shoulders, holding her in place, telling himself it was so she wouldn't slip again. But his mind and his heart were telling him something else as she lifted her gaze slowly to meet his.

"Michael…" Her voice trailed off and she licked her lips, making him wonder again about whether he'd kissed her last night.

Angela merely blinked up at him, trying to gather her thoughts. It was hard to talk, to think when he had his hands on her and was so close, close enough she could feel his sweet, warm breath grazing her skin.

Still feeling unsteady, and not certain if it was from the icy ground, or his closeness, Angela lifted a hand to his chest. "Michael, I…" She couldn't seem to drag her gaze from his. He had such beautiful eyes, she thought. Beautiful and intense.

And he was looking at her with such longing of his own. Looking at her as if she were the only woman in the world; a beautiful, desirable woman. It had been so long since she'd felt that way it made her heart and body ache in a way it hadn't in years.

"Angela." Watching her, Michael felt as if some invisible force was drawing him closer and closer to her and he seemed incapable of stopping it. He was lost in her eyes, her scent, her entire being and he knew he shouldn't be, couldn't be.

He had far too much at risk to be playing with fire. And in the past twenty-four hours, he'd learned that Angela was like a flame that kept calling him, drawing him closer and closer. And he seemed utterly powerless to stop it.

But he knew he must.

"What Michael?" She licked her lips again, hanging on to his jacket, closing her fingers around the cold leather and hanging on for dear life.

He could feel himself sinking deeper as rational thought and reason fled, swept away by the tide of feelings, emotions and needs that her closeness, her presence, generated.

"Angela," he said again, lifting one hand to cup her cheek, knowing he should say something, but knowing also that his mind had emptied the moment he'd touched her.

He merely stared at her a moment before he lowered his head and brushed his lips against hers. Softly, as gentle as a whisper, his lips caressed and warmed hers, then, as the desire took hold, flaring bright and hot, he dragged her closer, took the kiss deeper, wanting only to squelch the flame that seemed about to burn out of control and incinerate them both.

She kissed him back, her lips shy, unsteady and a bit tentative, making him realize she probably had very little experience at this. Odd, considering she had a child.

His thoughts blurred and spun and he pulled her closer, wanting to feel the warmth and heat of her pressing against him, warming the chill that seemed buried in his heart.

Her hands slid from the front of his jacket to his neck, circling him, dragging him closer, letting her fingers feel the cool skin of his neck and the warm silk of his hair.

She went up on tiptoe, unaware that she was kissing him back as fiercely as he was kissing her. Right here in her driveway. In broad daylight, where anyone—her neighbors, her precious daughter or her uncle—could see.

Ludicrous, she thought for a moment, but did nothing to stop it, wanting only to feel this wonderful sense of aliveness that had eluded her until this moment, until Michael kissed her.

Heady and dizzy, Angela realized *this* was the excitement women knew, experienced and whispered about. The kind of wild whirlwind of inexplicable passion capable of taking a woman past sanity and over the brink.

"Mama?"

Angela froze at the sound of her daughter's voice. With regret, she drew back from Michael, then slowly unwound her arms from around him and carefully took a step away. Her lips tingled and her legs were like rubber. She feared her legs wouldn't hold her, and could only silently pray they would.

"Yes, honey?" Her voice was soft, shakier than she would have liked when she turned toward the house and saw Emma peeking out the back door. Not certain how much her daughter had seen, Angela's face flamed and she felt embarrassed at having been caught kissing a man. Her daughter had never so much as seen her touch a man before.

"Mama, the buzzer on the oven is going off." Emma stood coatless in the open doorway, shivering, with the dogs huddled protectively at her feet. "I don't know what to do. The dogs are howling 'cuz of the noise. Are you coming in now, Mama?"

"Right now, honey," Angela said, bending to pick up Michael's dropped coffee cup from the snow. "Go back inside and close the door, honey, before you catch cold." Angela couldn't bear to look at Michael, not certain what she'd see. "I've got to see to dinner," she said quietly, not even glancing at him as she carefully started toward the house, stepping gingerly so she wouldn't slip again, trying to forget the impact of his kiss.

Chapter Four

By late Friday afternoon, the ten inches of new snow the weatherman had been predicting became a reality. As the weekend continued, so did the snow, finally trickling off late Sunday afternoon, but not before more than seventeen additional inches of new snow had fallen, further tangling efforts to clear the streets and roadways.

The temperature dropped, hovering just above zero, while the wind picked up, howling bitterly through the countryside like a cyclone, sending prickles of ice and snow flying through the air like torpedoes.

As the county began the slow process of digging out, the elementary school telephone tree went to work, informing parents that classes had been cancelled the next day—for the fourth day in a row. The telephone tree listed three parents to call, the last person on the list called the next three and so on until word spread to everyone.

Bored, restless and unable to go out and play because of the weather, by late Sunday afternoon, Emma was growing increasingly bored and antsy.

Trying to get some much-needed quiet time to pay bills and tend to paperwork, Angela sent her daughter upstairs to her room to straighten it up.

One quick glance told Emma her room was straight enough, and she went in search of Michael. She found him in the kitchen, lying on his back, with his head stuck in the cabinet under the sink, muttering imprecations about pipes and plumbers under his breath.

"Michael?" Emma scrunched down on her haunches next to his prone body, trying to hear what he was muttering. "Who you talking to?"

"Hmm? Uh, no one, Em," he hedged. "I was just muttering to myself."

"What'cha doing?" Emma asked, trying to poke her head inside the darkened cabinet to see what he was doing.

"Trying to fix this leak in the pipes for your mother. Remember she told you how I'm going to be doing some maintenance and chores around the inn for her?"

"I remember," Emma said. "Why's the pipe leaking?" she asked, squinting hard to see inside the darkness and making Michael laugh.

"If I knew that, Em, I wouldn't have my head stuck in this cabinet, using words I'm sure your mother wouldn't approve of."

"What kind of words?" Emma asked.

"Never mind," Michael muttered. "Hey, Em?"

"Huh?"

"You want to be my helper today?"

Excitement brightened her eyes and she bounced up and down nearly toppling over. "Your helper? Really?"

"Really," he confirmed. "See that big old tool box there?"

She glanced around, crossing her legs comfortably underneath her as she sat down next to him, prepared to be helpful. "You mean this big metal box on the floor here?"

"That's it. Can you reach inside of it and grab me that big wrench?"

"I don't know what a wench is," she said, squinting at the mass of tangled tools in the box.

"Wrench, Em, not wench," he said in amusement. "It's real big and silver and funny shaped. It has a bright red handle. Do you know what color red is?"

She giggled, pushing her glasses up her nose. "'Course, I'm not a baby. I know my colors and the alphabet and I know how to read, too."

"Good girl. Now, can you lift that wrench up very carefully—use both hands, Em, it's heavy—and hand it to me?"

Using both hands, Emma bit her lip in concentration as she lifted the heavy tool and all but heaved it at Michael's open, outstretched palm.

"Thanks, hon," he said, pulling his hand back under the cabinet so he could continue.

"Michael?"

"Yeah?"

"How many more hours until Christmas?"

Still totally charmed by the unending curiosity and questions this child had, he slid out from under the cabinet to look at her.

"Hours?" he repeated with a lift of his brow, wonder-

ing how quickly he could do the math. Probably not quick enough to conceal that he was a complete math moron. "I'm not sure, honey. Lots and lots of hours." He thought for a moment. "But it's easier to figure it out in days or weeks." A thought brightened his face. "Em, does your mom have a calendar?"

"Yeah, there's a big one on the refrigerator. It's a doggy one. Mama bought it from the vet and keeps it on the 'frigerator to mark down all the stuff we have to do each day. She checks it every morning so she knows what we got to do." Her frown deepened, clouding her big blue eyes. "How come you want to know if we gots a calendar?"

"I'll show you. Why don't you go get it?" Michael said as Emma scrambled to her feet to do just that. "And get a red crayon while you're at it."

The crayon she brought back was more a stub than anything else, but it would do, Michael decided.

"Now, here's what you do, Em. See the day for today?"

Squinting behind her glasses, she examined the calendar. "Today's Sunday, right?"

"That's right," he said, sliding back under the cabinet and swearing softly when he whacked his elbow on a pipe.

"You said a bad word," Emma said, covering her mouth with her hand to hide a giggle.

"I know, Em. A very bad word." He lifted his head to wink at her. "But let's not tell your mom, okay?" he asked, wincing and imagining what Angela's reaction to his rather colorful language would be. "I don't want to get in trouble with your mom."

She giggled again, the idea of a big person being in trouble too funny to resist. "Okay, we won't tell Mama." She glanced down at the calendar. "What am I supposed to do again?"

"Find today on the calendar, Em," he said. "It's Sunday, and it should be about the fourth or fifth of December." Since he'd arrived, he'd sort of lost track of things like dates and times. One day seemed to flow pleasantly and comfortably into the next. It was surprising how peaceful and addictive the lack of stress in his life had become. It was something he was quickly getting used to.

The inn had afforded him the opportunity to feel as if all of his worries and cares had slipped away. The vague sense of unease and dissatisfaction he'd been feeling had lifted, leaving a sense of peace and contentment.

"I see it," Emma said, beaming. "It's the fifth of December, right?" she asked, keeping her finger pointed to the right day.

"That's right, Em."

"Okay, so now what?"

"Now you can figure out how many days until Christmas."

"How?" she asked with a deep frown.

"Well, Em, Christmas is on the twenty-fifth. Can you see that day on the calendar?"

Emma nodded, pleased and excited and all but bouncing up and down again. She loved Christmas more than anything in the world. "I see it. I see it. Mama put a big heart on that day so we wouldn't forget it's Christmas."

"Okay, so count how many days it is from today until Christmas day."

"Count?"

"Yep, just count."

She did, aloud, making Michael smile when she announced proudly, "It's only twenty days until Christmas if you don't count today."

"Exactly. Now here's what you do, Em. Got your red crayon?"

"Yep."

"Okay, put a big old red *X* over today's date."

"But why?" she asked, frowning.

He chuckled. "So you can see that this day has come, and that's one less day you have to wait for Christmas. Every day, you can put another big red *X* on the calendar, and then you'll always know, by counting from the big red *X*, how many days are left until Christmas."

"Cool," she said, beaming and seeing his logic. "So every morning before school I could count how many days are left until Christmas."

"Exactly."

"Michael?"

"Yeah, hon?"

"I've been saving my money for Christmas. I've got almost one dollar and sixty-four cents. I'm gonna buy Mama a Christmas present."

"You are?" Michael said. "What are you going to buy her?"

Emma frowned. "I don't know. She said all she needed was time, but I don't know where to buy that, do you?"

Michael chuckled. Sounded like just what a busy, single mother would want and need. From what he'd seen of Angela and the amount of work she did each and every day, taking care not just of the inn, but Emma and her uncle as well, Michael figured she could use some extra time. His admiration for her and the responsibilities she shouldered single-handedly every day grew with each passing day.

She was an incredible woman, he realized. And beautiful, he amended with a grin, knowing he'd best keep that opinion to himself. "Sorry, hon, I don't have a clue where you can buy that, either."

"I'm gonna buy Uncle Jimmy something—"

"Emma Marie." Angela came to a halt, her hand still on the swinging door as she caught sight of her daughter, sitting on the floor, chattering away to Michael. "Are you supposed to be bothering Michael when he's working? Didn't we just have this conversation yesterday *and* the day before?" Angela asked with a lift of her brow, trying not to let her exasperation show. "And didn't I tell you to go upstairs and straighten your room?"

Eyes wide, Emma scrambled to her feet. "Mama, my room's straightened and I'm not bothering Michael. Honest," she protested with a pout, glancing toward Michael for support. "I'm helping him."

"Helping him?" Angela repeated dubiously, letting the door swing shut behind her as she came into the kitchen. Try as she might, she had been unable to keep her daughter away from Michael. Emma followed him around like a lost puppy, seeking his company, attention and approval. And Michael, whom she'd discovered had the patience of a saint, especially when it came to inquisitive little girls, seemed to relish in Emma's devotion. Not once had he become irritable or impatient with her. He was gentle and kind and took his time to talk to Emma—really talk to her—as if she were a person, not just a kid.

And, Angela had to admit, he'd impressed the hell out of her more and more each and every day. But then again, what mother wouldn't find her heart softening toward a man who was so kind and patient with her child?

Desperately trying to keep her defenses up, Angela glanced at Michael, still lying on the floor, his long, muscled legs stretched out in front of him, his work shirt pulled taut against his body as he lifted his hands over his head to do something under the sink.

Angela ground her teeth together and let her eyes slide closed for a moment, trying not to think about all those tight, gorgeous muscles of his. The man could tempt a saint, she thought, trying not to stare at him. She couldn't see his face, but she didn't have to; she knew it practically by heart now. Every square inch of it—not just from seeing him every day, but from seeing that face in her dreams every night, as well.

"Honest, Mama. Ask him," Emma implored.

"She's right, Angela," Michael said, grabbing his rag and his tools before sliding out from under the sink. He wiped his grimy hands, then glanced at Angela and felt a quick surge of desire whack him nearly senseless. She looked terrific, he thought with a grin. Today, she had on a sweatsuit the color of grass. The baggy, shapeless garment did little to conceal her feminine curves or her beauty.

Her long dark hair was pulled back into a ponytail that sat high on her head, making her look almost as young as a teenager. A few wisps had sprung free, framing her face.

Her face was clear of makeup and so dewy soft and delectable that his fingers itched to reach out and touch it. He'd scrupulously avoided doing just that—touching her—since he'd kissed her out by the shed the other day.

That kiss had knocked him for a loop and he needed some time to get his bearings, to put things in perspective. He still wasn't certain he'd done that—yet. He wasn't a man who went blindly down a path without knowing the consequences. In his job, it had become a necessity if he wanted to stay alive. He was no less cautious in his personal life, knowing exactly what an ill-fated mistake could cost him.

"I asked Em to be my helper today." He glanced down at Emma and grinned, his heart all but melting. This kid had wormed her way into his heart, capturing it as surely as if she'd lassoed it. He shrugged and continued wiping his hands, aware that Angela was watching him carefully, but she'd been doing that since he'd arrived. He figured sooner or later she was going to learn she had nothing to be wary or suspicious about with him. "I figured since she doesn't have school she might as well be my helper and earn some money for Christmas." He winked at Emma who beamed up at him, her eyes dancing in excitement. "It's only twenty days away, right, Em?"

Emma's eyes widened into saucers. "I'm going to get paid to help you?" she asked, thrilled at the possibility and responsibility.

"Of course," he confirmed, giving one of her pigtails an affectionate tug. "When you work, you get paid. It's a simple but effective plan," he explained with a laugh, glancing at Angela again. "It's always worked for me." He went down on his haunches so that he was at eye-level with Emma. "Now hon, one of the things you need to learn if you're going to be my helper is that you always have to put things back where they belong when you're done with them."

"You mean, I have to go put the crayon back and hang up the calendar now?"

"That's right, sweetheart," he said with an approving nod. "That way tomorrow, when you want to count the days until Christmas, you'll know right where the calendar and your crayon are and you won't have to spend time hunting them up." He glanced at Angela, his eyes twinkling in amusement. "I showed her how to easily count the days until Christmas."

"Good idea," Angela said, impressed again. The man was full of surprises. Gorgeous. Kind. Gentle. And practical. Something about him kept pulling her toward him in spite of her very practical reasons to stay away from him. And having him here, underfoot everyday, charming her, her daughter and her uncle wasn't helping the situation any. "I'm sorry I didn't think of that," she said, remembering how Emma asked almost every single day. "How long until Christmas?"

He shrugged. "It's an old trick of my grandfather's. When my siblings and I were younger, apparently each of us asked him almost every day how long until Christmas, and with seven of us, I imagine it got a bit tedious. So he devised this system. We each had our own calendars to hang in our room so we'd know how many days until Christmas, or whatever big day we were anxiously waiting for."

"Your grandfather sounds like a very wise man," Angela said with a smile.

"Oh, he is," Michael said, laughing. "But don't ever tell him that or there'd be no living with him."

"I'll go put my stuff away." Emma bent and grabbed the crayon off the floor and then scooped up the calendar, hugging it to her tightly before glancing up at Michael. "Are you still gonna teach me to play checkers tonight?"

Michael nodded. "Absolutely. Right after dinner."

She grinned and then frowned. "Uncle Jimmy says I'm too little to learn to play."

"Can you tell the difference between red and black?" Michael asked, going down on his haunches again and laying a gentle hand on her shoulder. She nodded vigorously. "Great. Then that's all you need to know in order to play checkers."

"Cool." Still grinning, Emma glanced at her mother, relieved to see her "mad" face was gone. "Do you need help with anything else right now?"

Michael shook his head. "No, not right now, pint-size. I'll handle putting my wrench and rag away," he said, dropping the wrench back into the box with a little thud. "Go on and put that stuff away and I'll see you later."

With a happy nod, Emma skipped out of the kitchen, grinning broadly at her mother as she passed.

"You know, Michael, with the patience you have with children, maybe you should have been a teacher." Angela smiled and then moved toward the stove to check on the pork she had roasting for dinner.

"A teacher?" Michael said, all but shuddering. "I can handle little people one on one, but I'm not so sure how I'd do when I'm outnumbered by them."

"Oh, I don't know about that. I don't think you give yourself enough credit." He was absolutely amazing with children. Just amazing, she thought as she grabbed a pot holder to open the oven door. She'd never seen anyone who was as natural with children as he was.

"That leak under the sink is fixed. I think," he added with a slight frown as he pulled the maintenance list of chores that needed to be done from the back pocket of his jeans and marked it off. Once Jimmy had agreed to let him work off his room and board over the next month, they'd gone through the entire inn, room by room, with the list of chores that needed to be done. Michael planned to tackle all of those before even starting the preparations for the Christmas festival, which thankfully wasn't for three more weeks.

Something caught his attention and he glanced up, sniffing deeply. "Whatever you're cooking smells terrific," he said, coming up behind Angela, not certain which smelled better—her or her dinner. He'd been trying to keep his distance, to give her some distance, and he had to admit, it was driving him crazy. The urge to touch her, to hold her and kiss her again was a constant annoyance, one he'd dutifully tried to ignore.

"Thanks," she said, basting the roast, then pushing the oven rack back in. "But you say that every day, Michael." She straightened and turned, surprised to find him standing directly behind her. She froze for an instant, her eyes, those wary beautiful eyes shifting to his.

"You know," he said quietly. "A guy might take it personally the way you always freeze up and look so suspicious and wary whenever he gets close."

Knowing it was true, but not wanting to admit it, Angela shrugged. "I'm sorry, I don't know what you're talking about."

Since he'd arrived, the more comfortable Emma had become around him, the more increasingly nervous and uncomfortable Angela had become around him. Perhaps it was because she knew the power he had, what his touch was capable of doing to her.

Since he'd rescued her from her fall the other day out by the toolshed, then kissed her silly, she'd steadfastly tried not to be alone with him for any reason. She avoided any hint of any personal conversation or any kind of personal interaction.

There was nothing *personal* between them, she reminded herself firmly. He was a guest, nothing more, and regardless of how he made her feel when he touched her, it wouldn't change the fact that she wasn't in the least bit interested in a *personal* relationship with him—or any other man.

"Ah, Angela, I think something's happening here," Michael said calmly, leaning forward until he was almost nose to nose with her.

"W-what?" she said nervously, drawing back. His masculine scent teased and taunted her, reminding her what it felt like to be close to him, to hold him, to kiss him. Steadfastly, she banished the thought. "I don't know what you're talking about," she said again.

With a small smile, he gently skimmed his finger down her nose. "Seems to me your nose is growing." His smile became a full grin as she frowned, then blushed in embarrassment. "It has a tendency to do that whenever someone tells a fib, like you just did," he reminded her. "Lying doesn't become you, Angela," he said softly. "For now, we'll just leave it at that, but I'm not the kind of man who likes to be lied to." He straightened his frame. "For now, we'll just pretend that you're not wary and suspicious of me. Maybe once you get to know me better, you'll come to realize you have no reason to be, either." He reached out a hand and tucked a strand of hair behind her ear, as she did her best not to stiffen. "Some people think I'm a pretty nice guy." He smiled. "Maybe someday you will, too."

Whistling softly, Michael slipped his hands into his pockets, then pushed through the swinging doors of the kitchen, leaving Angela staring wide-eyed after him.

* * *

Grateful to have a few minutes alone to gather her composure, Angela went about doing her usual Sunday chores in preparation for the week ahead.

She always considered Sundays her day off. Not that she didn't work; she did, but just at a much slower pace than the weekdays required. Dressed comfortably and warm in a sweatsuit—which she considered her day-off relaxing attire, and with her hair pulled back into a ponytail, she quickly finished up the last of the breakfast dishes, then cleaned the rest of the kitchen.

On Sundays, she always planned her menu for the coming week, cooking as much as possible and then freezing the food so that no matter how busy or frazzled she was during the week, she was always able to provide home-cooked meals for her family and guests.

In the six years since she'd taken over the management of the inn, she'd learned that organization and planning were the keys to being a successful businesswoman and a single working mother.

Although summer was their busiest time, the inn was usually always full from midApril through the first of November. However, Angela made sure that she always put Emma and her needs first. It wasn't always easy and required lots of late nights and juggling. But she knew that nothing in the world was more important than her daughter or her daughter's happiness.

Which was perhaps why Michael made her so nervous, she thought. She wasn't interested in having any kind of relationship with a man. She simply didn't have time, nor did she want any further complications in her life; but that didn't mean she wasn't human and didn't have feelings.

She *had* feelings, lots of normal, female feelings that Michael had stirred up once again after six long years of dormancy, which was probably why he made her so nervous.

But that didn't mean she couldn't keep things on a professional level; she could, as long as she controlled those feelings and the impulses that went along with them. She knew that this time, it wasn't merely her heart or her pride at stake; this time, she had to consider her precious daughter, as well.

Reminding herself of her responsibility to Emma, Angela headed into the living room to start her chores in there, certain she'd be able to handle Michael as long as she stayed aware of and alert to her own feelings and the danger his presence added to her heart and her everyday life.

With a weary sigh, Michael pushed away from his desk and stood up, pressing his hands to his tired eyes. It was dark and late—after midnight—and he'd been writing for hours.

Stifling a yawn, he walked to the window and stared out into the night's darkness, rubbing his aching shoulder. He'd plowed snow this afternoon again and chopped more wood; now his muscles were reminding him just how long it had been since he'd been doing any physical work regularly.

But he found, to his delight, that he really enjoyed doing physical work. It had been a long time since he'd used his brawn, as opposed to his brains, and he found it more relaxing than he'd ever imagined.

Gone was the vague sense of dissatisfaction that had been dogging him for the past few years, the frustration of knowing no matter how hard he worked, the crooks and the crooked would be back out on the street, plying their trade and their tricks, within days, or even hours, of their arrest.

That frustration had been replaced by the satisfaction of having accomplished a job and being able to see the results. The long, winding driveway that led to the inn was now clear of mountains of snow, and just inside the shed was enough firewood to last through the next few days until the delivery truck could get through.

Standing at the window, dressed in jeans and a sweatshirt, he gazed out into the darkness, realizing he was pleasantly sleepy.

He'd been making good use of his time, he reasoned, writing and doing all the things Angela needed him to do.

Tonight he'd retired to his room around eight, right about the time Emma went to bed, to do some writing and had gotten so caught up in it, he hadn't realized how late it really was.

His eyes were tired, the muscles in his neck tense and his fingertips were all but raw from all the typing he'd been doing; but it all came with such a deep sense of satisfaction that he couldn't even begin to complain.

He was happy, he realized with a silly grin, leaning against the window jamb. Very happy. And more importantly, content with his life for the first time in a very long time. He knew that both Emma and Angela had a lot to do with it.

Funny, he usually never spent much time thinking— brooding, his grandfather called it—until he'd come to the inn. Maybe because until he'd met Angela and Emma, he'd had no reason to question his decisions.

But now, after they had aroused and stirred feelings and longings he'd never even been aware of, he found himself longing for things—things he'd never considered a possibility before.

Everything here was so different from what his life had been like—he was different, he realized, and perhaps that's what the big change really amounted to. Stress was almost nonexistent here at the inn, as was the worry and accompanying physical problems he'd been experiencing the past few years—the sleeplessness, the lack of appetite, the constantly being on guard. It had all dissipated, leaving him feeling better, physically and emotionally, than he had in years.

Rejuvenated, he realized, yawning and stretching his arms over his head as he continued to stare into the dark Wisconsin night. He felt completely rejuvenated.

There were two soft thumps at the door and Michael glanced at his bedside clock.

"Right on time, boys," he muttered as he went to the door and opened it. "Well, are you going to just stand there or come in?" he asked the two dogs who stared up at him woefully for a moment.

"Well, come on," he urged, ushering them in with a sweep of his hand. They trotted into the room and then made themselves comfortable, stretching out on the carpet.

He still couldn't tell Mackenzie from Mahoney, but apparently they didn't mind. Sometime during the last week, they'd stopped growling at him and had accepted that he was merely just a kindred spirit who was always good for a handout of food. Soon they had started following him around like lovesick…puppies.

"You're just hoping for some of those cookies from dinner, aren't you, boys?" he muttered, reaching down to give their heads a pat. "Spoiled rotten, both of you," he accused with a shake of his head. "All right, come on, we'll go raid the kitchen. But I'm warning you, you have to be quiet tonight. No swooning and making goo-goo sounds over cookies again," he scolded as he walked out of his room in his stocking feet and quietly shut the door behind him. He glanced up the stairs, just to make sure the coast was clear.

"Now be quiet, both of you," he ordered in a whisper, putting his finger to his lips as if the canines understood what he was saying. "You'll give us away with all those doggy noises."

Last night, he'd slipped the two mutts several pieces of Angela's fresh baked oatmeal cookies left over from dinner and ended up shushing both of them when they all but howled and rolled their eyes in pleasure.

He knew the feeling. Angela's cooking nearly had him howling and swooning every day.

Silently, the three of them trotted downstairs together. Absently, Michael rubbed his chest through his sweatshirt; his spurt of physical activity had gone a long way toward easing the aches and pains that had remained from his accident. The bruise on his chest had finally faded, and the cut on his forehead was now just a memory.

He pushed through the swinging kitchen door, all but fighting the dogs to get through first.

"Angela." Stunned, he came to an abrupt halt, causing the dogs to all but barrel right into him. She was sitting at the kitchen table in the dark, but the night-light in the hall cascaded through the open doorway, shadowing her in a faint yellow glow.

Caught, he glanced guiltily at the two dogs who looked up at him with innocent, wide eyes.

"Mmm, yes, Angela," she said, getting to her feet with a smile. She had on warm plaid flannel slippers and a heavy quilted floor-length robe that revealed little of her figure.

Still, knowing that she was no doubt dressed in her nightclothes caused Michael's blood to sizzle. There was nothing wrong with his imagination, and he could well imagine what she looked like under all that heavy plaid and quilting. She crossed her arms across her breasts and stared at the three of them.

"I figured they had to be keeping someone company since the past few nights when I've come down to let them out for the night, they've been missing in action, so to speak."

"Uh…we…uh…they…" At a loss, Michael glared down at the dogs. "You could help me out here," he muttered to them, making Angela laugh.

"Well, at least now I know where they've been each night." Angela smiled at the dogs as she headed toward the back door and opened it. Both dogs merely stood there, looking at her as if waiting for Michael's permission. "Well?" she said with a lift of her brow. The wind whipped wickedly, and Angela shivered as the cold air blew in through the door, chilling her.

"Go on, boys," Michael encouraged, giving one of them a gentle nudge with his knee. "Go out and when you get back you can have your midnight snack."

The dogs hesitated for just a moment, before trotting toward the door one behind the other. They paused and looked back at him once last time.

"Go on," he encouraged, shooing them with his hand. "I'll wait for you." They trotted through the open door into the backyard and Angela quickly closed the door behind them, shaking her head with a laugh. "Seems to me you've got your own fan club."

"They just know I'm a soft touch when it comes to

cookies." Michael frowned. "How come you're up, Angela?" he asked, watching as she went to the cabinet and took down a plate, then filled it with fresh oatmeal cookies.

She shrugged. "I couldn't sleep." Because she couldn't stop thinking about him, she thought but didn't add as she brought the plate to the table. "And you?"

He grinned and pulled out a chair. "I was writing. Didn't realize just how late it was."

"How's it going?" she asked softly, aware that she might be prying. Cocking her head, she studied him. "Have you been able to get any writing done? You've been doing a lot of work around here and spending a lot of time with Emma, and I didn't know if you'd actually been able to get any writing done."

She knew he disappeared every evening right about the time she put Emma to bed, so she'd assumed he'd been writing. Although she hadn't asked him about it, she had been curious.

"It's going well," he admitted, feeling a rush of pride. "Very well. I've really gotten a handle on the story, I think. I've got the entire outline completed. A few more hours tonight and it should be done."

"What happens after you write the outline?"

He blew out a breath. "Then I start actually writing the story." He hesitated. "I don't know if this is the way other writers work, but in college I had a professor who was absolutely fanatical about outlining. Claimed trying to write a book without an outline was like trying to drive from Miami to L.A. without a road map."

She chuckled. "That doesn't sound like fun."

"No, nor is it very practical." He shrugged. "So now that

I know I've got a beginning, a middle and an ending, I guess it's time to write the actual story." He didn't want to admit that he felt a mixture of both fear and excitement, wondering if he could really do it. But the story and the characters were so alive for him—almost as if they were real people he knew—that he was anxious to see if he could transfer those feelings onto the printed page.

"Michael?" she began hesitantly. "Would you let me read it? Your story?"

Surprise shifted over his features and he stared at her for a moment. "You want to read it?"

She shrugged. "If you don't mind. I've never met a writer before, so I don't know how they or you feel about having someone read your work, but I do read a lot, mostly women's fiction and mysteries. No horror, though," she specified with a shake of her head. "I don't want to be scared out of my wits," she added with a chuckle. "But I really enjoy reading."

"I'd be happy to let you read it, Angela, but it's on disk. I don't have my printer with me so I can't print out the pages."

"Why don't you use the inn's printer?" she asked. "Remember the day we went through the maintenance list, and I printed that page out for you?" He nodded. "Well, the printer's in that covered cabinet right next to the computer. You're more than welcome to use it at any time."

"Yeah?" he said with a grin, more pleased than he believed possible. He never knew for sure how anything "fit" until he actually read it in hard copy. Holding the pages in his hands somehow made it seem more real to him.

"Yeah." She grinned.

"Great. I'll do that." He reached for a cookie, bit into it and nearly swooned. "These are fabulous."

"Thanks." She frowned a bit. "Michael, I wanted to mention that tomorrow afternoon I have an appointment in town. Even though school's been cancelled because of the snow, Emma has a play date here with her friend, Barbie, in the afternoon, so I'm going to call our regular babysitter to come and stay with the girls."

"Why?" Michael asked with a frown, reaching for another cookie.

"Why what?"

"Why on earth are you going to pay a babysitter when Jimmy and I will both be here?" His face clouded a moment. "Or don't you trust us with the girls?" he asked, trying not to feel hurt.

"No," she said, shaking her head. "I trust you. It's just Uncle Jimmy won't be here. He's got a doctor's appointment in town."

"Yeah, okay, so I'll watch the girls."

"You?" she repeated, trying not to smile. "Alone?"

One brow lifted. "Don't think I can handle two little girls for a couple of hours?"

"No, it's not that. It's just that…babysitting isn't exactly part of the deal. And I certainly don't expect you to do it."

He shrugged and reached for another cookie, before getting up to let the dogs back in. They stood on their carpet and shook themselves, spraying cold, wet snow over Michael.

"Hey, watch it," he scolded, stamping his foot and stepping off the carpet so his socks wouldn't get any wetter. He turned back to Angela. "So what? Don't you think I can handle it?"

There was a challenge in his eye and Angela had a feeling this was another one of those macho-male-ego things.

"No, of course not."

"I mean, come on Angela, I'm an adult. It's not like I can't handle a couple of little girls for a few hours."

If he wanted to handle the girls, well then, she'd let him handle them. And then she'd clean up the mess afterward, to be sure. "Are you sure?" she asked hesitantly.

"Positive." He sat back down, crumbling up a couple of pieces of cookies and giving them to the dogs who sat hovering at his heels. "It'll be fun."

She laughed. "Tell me that when it's over, Michael. Then we'll see how much fun it was."

"Piece of cake," he muttered, stuffing another cookie in his mouth. He glanced up at her, aware she was watching him. "What's wrong?" he asked, realizing something was shadowing those beautiful eyes of hers.

"Michael. I owe you an apology."

He frowned. "For what?"

"For this morning. I lied to you this morning, Michael," Angela said. "I…I…told you this morning that you didn't make me wary or nervous, and that's not quite the truth." She lifted her gaze to his, held it in spite of the fact that just looking at him—looking at that gorgeous face, those eyes, that mouth—made her long for things she knew better than to long for. "I wasn't being honest with you, Michael," she said softly. "And that's not like me."

He reached across the table and lifted her chin, feeling his own bout of guilt. If the truth be told, he wasn't being totally honest with her, either. "I know, Angela," he said softly. "But I figured you'd realize sooner or later that you've got nothing to fear from me."

"Perhaps," she agreed hesitantly, forcing herself to meet his gaze again. "But I don't have a right to lie to you. And

I did." She shook her head. "I'm sorry, Michael, truly, as far as I'm concerned there is never a legitimate reason to lie to someone. People do it when they're afraid of the consequences or facing the truth, and I'm sorry, but that's simply not acceptable to me. And I apologize. You were right. You do make me wary, nervous and suspicious," she added with a shaky laugh. "But it's only because I haven't had, or allowed myself to have, any kind of relationship or feelings for a man since my divorce."

"I understand," he said carefully. As a general rule, he agreed with her, and had pretty much lived his life the same way—truthfully. Until now. Now he knew he was breaking all his own rules about being honest, but he knew there simply was no other way, not just for his own selfish reasons, he assured himself, but for her and Emma's safety and protection. He couldn't tell them the truth—not without risking exposing himself and perhaps them, to danger, something he simply wasn't willing to do.

He willingly chose his career, knew the inherent risks and dangers, but Emma and Angela were innocent bystanders and there was no way he had a right to put them in harm's way, no matter how remote the possibility.

"No, Michael you don't understand," she said quietly, forcing herself to keep her gaze level with his. "For some odd reason...there's something about you that... I don't know how to explain it, Michael, but whenever you're near me, it seems as if I lose all common sense and reason." Putting her actual feelings into words embarrassed her and she could feel the blush climb her cheeks.

Delighted, he grinned, brushing a wayward strand of hair off her cheek. "I know the feeling, Angela. You do the same thing to me," he admitted. Until this moment, until he'd actually put what he'd been feeling into words, he hadn't realized just how strong his feelings for Angela and Emma were.

His words only seemed to further alarm Angela, judging by the look that crossed her face. "But the difference between us Michael, is that I'm not interested in having a relationship, not with anyone, especially a man. And I certainly am not interested in a fling. I can't afford it, not emotionally, and I certainly can't afford the time. I have my hands full with Emma and the inn, and my uncle. I just don't have the time or the energy to get involved with any man," she said firmly, lifting her gaze to his. "I've rebuilt my life here, one of stability and security for myself and my daughter, a life where nothing can ever hurt or harm either of us again, and I can't afford to do anything that might risk everything I've built for us. Do you understand?"

He understood fear, at least her fear; he could see it in her eyes, all but feel it vibrating off her body, but that didn't mean because he understood it that he liked it.

Wounded, he thought sadly. Angela had been badly wounded, and now was hovering over her daughter in a protective gesture meant to keep them both safe and he couldn't help but wonder why. It only made all his protective urges toward them come out full force. He could never willingly do anything to hurt them, not now, not ever.

Which was precisely why he couldn't tell her the truth about who he was or why he was here.

"Sure, but Angela, I don't know what I did to make you think I was interested in a fling." He stroked a finger down her cheek, wanting to soothe, to erase some of that fear from her eyes. "I'm sorry if I did something to offend you," he said quietly. "That wasn't my intention."

"I didn't mean that you had. It's just that I don't want there to be any misunderstandings. I have Emma and my life here, and my work and, quite frankly, I don't have anything to offer you. Nothing except perhaps my friendship." It was a lie; she knew it. She wanted, she yearned to be able to have more—with him. Michael was everything she'd always imagined, wished for and wanted in a man. A mate. A father for her child. But she knew that her own past mistakes, trusting the wrong man, prevented it. She couldn't—wouldn't—let her heart override her intellect. Not ever, ever again. For Emma's sake.

Friendship. Michael shifted as the word rang over and over in his mind like a mantra. Until this moment, he'd always rather liked that word. Now it had a very empty, hollow ring to it and he wasn't certain why.

With a wistful sigh that started somewhere deep inside his own, wounded lonely heart, Michael realized Angela was everything in the world he'd ever thought he'd wanted or needed. Everything he'd always dreamed of before he'd put those dreams aside. And it frightened him probably as much as it did her.

"Friendship, huh?" he repeated. "Well, it seems to me, Angela, that a man couldn't ask for more than that."

Relieved, and yet somehow vaguely disappointed, she smiled at him. "Really?"

He brought her hand to his mouth and kissed her, resisting the urge to pull her to her feet and drag him to her for a real kiss, the kind that would curl her toes and singe her heart. She wasn't ready yet, he thought sadly. And he wasn't quite certain he was, either.

"Really," he confirmed with a nod as he kissed her hand again. For now at least, he thought to himself, and glanced at her. They'd be just friends. For now.

Chapter Five

The next day, Michael spent most of the morning working from the list of maintenance chores Angela had given him. By early afternoon, Jimmy had left for his doctor's appointment and Angela had departed for her appointment in town, but not without giving Michael a detailed list of instructions on how to care for the girls. Angela's worries almost made him smile.

If he could handle the dregs of the underground drug world of Chicago, he was pretty sure he could handle two little six-year-old girls for a couple of hours. But considering the circumstances, he certainly wasn't about to point that out to Angela.

Confident that he had everything under control, Michael went back to his work. He decided to work on the second floor, so he could be close to Emma's room where the girls were playing, just in case they needed him.

Humming quietly to himself, he thought about everything he'd accomplished today. He'd replaced washers in the guest bathroom sinks, replaced light bulbs in all the guest closets and replaced batteries in all the inn's smoke detectors. He'd repaired door locks and window hinges, and he'd even taken a stab at caulking one of the tubs in the guest baths to prevent water from leaking through the floor to the rooms below. He wasn't particularly skilled in plumbing, but knew enough to handle a few small plumbing tasks; knowing that gave him a profound sense of accomplishment.

Tomorrow he planned to start scraping the outdoor patio furniture in order to prepare the patio sets for a fresh coat of paint, which he hoped to complete by the end of next week, weather permitting. If Mother Nature didn't cooperate, he planned to move the furniture into the shed, if necessary, in order to complete the job in preparation for the Christmas festival.

Things were going along swimmingly, he mused, humming softly as he knelt in front of one of the guest rooms, the door ajar as he examined a broken lock.

He was just slipping the old, broken lock out of the doorframe when he heard a commotion coming from Emma's room.

"He did not."

"He did so."

"You're lying."

"Am not!"

"Are too!"

"I'm not a liar. You are. And you're a baby, too!"

"I am not a baby!"

"Baby, baby, you're a baby."

"And you're a liar! Liar, liar, pants on fire!"

It wasn't until he heard a loud crash, followed by a high-pitched scream and then the howls of both dogs, that Michael dropped the drill in his hand and took off for Emma's room in a near panic, almost tripping over his own feet as he took off at a run.

The door was partially ajar and he gently pushed it open. The floor was strewn with dolls and doll clothes, and in the middle was a dollhouse that looked as if it had barely survived an attempt at demolition.

The girls were standing face-to-face in the middle of the room, their tiny faces screwed into masks of fury as they glared at each other with clenched fists.

"Hey, hey, what's going on in here?" he asked.

He stepped deeper into the room, gingerly stepping over dolls and clothes, and bent to right the dollhouse, positioning himself directly between the two girls.

"Barbie said I'm a liar," Emma complained. Her glasses were askew, her pigtails were crooked, and her lower lip was trembling as her eyes filled with tears. Michael resisted the urge to rush to her, grab her up in his arms and protect her from all harm.

"Don't cry, Em," he said nervously, reaching in the back pocket of his jeans for his handkerchief, then giving it to her. "Please don't cry."

"She said I was a baby," Barbie accused, crossing her arms across her chest and glaring at Emma. "And I'm not a baby!" she declared fiercely, glaring up at Michael.

"And I'm not a liar!" Emma said, turning to Michael with tears welling in her big blue eyes. "Tell her I'm not a liar, Michael. Tell her I'm really your helper and that you're gonna pay me real money so I could buy Christmas presents."

"He is not!" Barbie declared, making a face at Emma, then sticking her tongue out at her for emphasis.

"Wait! Wait!" Michael held up his hand. "Stop this, you two. You're supposed to be friends and friends don't lie or call each other names, do they, Em?" he asked, looking directly at her and watching her lower lip tremble even more. Tears filled her eyes, but he held his ground. "Em?" he prompted softly, going down on one knee and slipping an arm around her. "Friends don't call each other names or tell each other lies, do they?"

"Uh-uh," she sniffled, swiping at her nose with his handkerchief.

"That's right," he confirmed with a nod, glancing at the still-glaring Barbie. "And Barbie, Em's not lying," he said, making the redheaded moppet's eyes widen. "Em's telling the truth." He glanced from one child to the other, wondering if maybe he was out of his depth in the face of such female fury—pint-size or not. "I really did ask Em to be my helper and I really am going to pay her real money."

"Told you," Emma said, sticking her own tongue out at Barbie.

"Em," Michael said. "That's not very nice."

"But she did it first," Emma protested.

"I know, but that's still not nice." He slid his other arm around Barbie, pulling her close, as well. "Now, Em, Barbie's your best friend and your guest, and I don't think your mom would be very happy to know that you were being rude to her, would she?" he asked.

Properly chastised, Emma wrapped her arms around him and burrowed her face into his shoulder. "No," she sniffled, swiping her wet, tear-stained face back and forth against the soft flannel of his shirt.

"And Barbie, Emma is your best friend. Do you think your mom would like it if she knew you were calling her a liar?"

Suitably chastised as well, the little redhead bowed her head. "No," she muttered, daring a glance at him through lowered lids.

"I didn't think so." He hesitated a moment, glancing from one child to the other, letting them think about what they'd done and said. "I think you both should apologize," he said quietly. "You're best friends, girls, and even friends get angry at one another sometimes, but there's never a reason to deliberately be mean to someone or to hurt them, especially your friends," he added gently, causing both girls to look guiltily at one another. "That's not the way you're supposed to treat friends."

"I'm sorry, Barbie," Emma said, after a gentle nudge from Michael.

"Me, too," Barbie said with a loud sniffle before swiping her nose along the length of one skinny, freckled arm.

"I didn't mean to call you a baby," Emma said with a grin.

"And you're not a liar, Em," Barbie offered with a matching grin of her own.

Satisfied that he'd averted a disaster, Michael grinned, giving them both a quick, approving hug. "I'm very proud of you, girls. It's always important to apologize when you're wrong, or when you've hurt someone, deliberate or not. And we don't tell lies to our friends, ever, do we?"

Tears welled in Emma's eyes as she shook her head. "No," she said softly, her voice barely a shaky whisper. At Michael's nod, Emma turned to her best friend. "I'm sorry,

Barbie, I didn't mean to hurt your feelings." She gave her best friend a hug, reaching across Michael and nearly squishing him in the process.

"Me, too, Em. I'm sorry," Barbie said, hugging Emma back. "You're still my bestest friend in the world," Barbie confirmed with a grin.

"And you're mine," Emma confirmed with a sniffle and a grin of her own.

Michael heaved a sigh of relief, until he glanced up and saw Angela standing in the doorway.

"Uh…uh…hi…Angela," he said, trying to hide his surprise and embarrassment.

"Hi, yourself," she said casually, letting her gaze shift from Michael to her daughter, then back again. "Problem?" she asked with a lift of her brow.

Michael glanced from Emma to Barbie. "Is there a problem, girls?" he asked meaningfully.

Sniffling, Emma wiped at her damp red eyes, then shook her head, sending her pigtails flying as she struggled to hide Michael's handkerchief behind her back so her mother wouldn't see it. "No, Mama, we don't got a problem," she replied with wide-eyed innocence.

"You sure about that?" Angela asked with the age-old wisdom every mother has when trouble is brewing.

"Honest." Emma glanced at Barbie. "Me and Barbie was just…just…" She glanced up at Michael for help.

"They were just learning some of the rules of friendship, right, girls?" he asked and they both nodded in unison.

"I see," Angela said carefully. It had been far too quiet when she'd come in the house, so she had naturally come upstairs to investigate. She'd been standing just outside the door while Michael had negotiated the situation, and she had to admit, he'd done an admirable job of it, as good as she could have done, if not a bit more diplomatically.

Something about seeing him with his arm around her daughter, comforting her and yet teaching her something that was both important and necessary to help her become a good person, had touched her heart, tugging on it until it felt as if it had simply melted.

"Well, then, if there's no problem, I think I'll go downstairs and unpack my groceries. Why don't you and Barbie clean up your toys and then come down and have a snack?"

"Okay, Mama," Emma said.

"I'll see you downstairs," Angela said, turning to leave the room, figuring she'd give Michael a chance to finish his conversation with the girls.

"Girls," Michael said after Angela left, "are you sure you're going to be all right?"

They both nodded. "Michael, I'm sorry we was fighting," Emma said, tears welling in her eyes again. "Mama said I was supposed to be good and I wasn't."

"Oh, sweetheart," Michael said, drawing her to him, hugging her tight. "You're always good, so don't cry. And even best friends fight sometimes. Heck, me and my brothers used to fight all the time but that didn't mean we didn't love each other." He grinned, gently pushing Emma's glasses back up her nose and swiping away a tear. "Now clean up this mess and I'll see you downstairs." He gave her a kiss on the forehead and then decided to go downstairs to face the music—and Angela.

Rubbing her throbbing temples, Angela carefully unloaded her first two bags of groceries, setting everything either on the counter or the kitchen table, depending on where it went.

After a frustrating afternoon arguing with the county tax assessor over the base figure he'd used to calculate the new property tax rate on the inn, she had not come home in the best of moods. Because of the snowstorms, everyone had been cooped up at home for days, so traffic in town had been a nightmare. Tempers had been short, so it had taken twice as long as she'd planned to do every errand, which only frustrated her more. By the time she'd pulled into the long winding drive of the inn, she'd had a raging headache.

Once she'd gotten the back door open—after nearly dropping the bag with the five dozen eggs—she'd stepped into the house, realizing it was quiet. Too quiet. Trying not to panic, she'd simply set the bags on the table and headed upstairs, where she realized a major battle had just concluded.

She stayed outside Emma's room waiting, listening, making certain Michael hadn't needed any reinforcements. He'd surprised her with the way he'd handled the situation. The man was, she thought again, a natural with children.

"What? Were you worried there'd be a run on eggs?" Michael asked with a lift of his brow as he pushed through the swinging doors of the kitchen and saw the dozens of eggs on the table.

"No," Angela said with a smile. "They're for the Christmas festival. Cookies," she clarified at his frown as he grabbed a bag of groceries and began to help her unload. "Every year, I swear I'm going to get a head start on my baking and every year something comes up and I get behind. This year, I'm determined to get started early." She opened the refrigerator and made room inside for the eggs before turning to face Michael.

"You don't have to help with that, Michael," she said as he lifted five pounds of sugar and flour into the cabinet for her.

He shrugged. "It's no big deal. I'm standing right here." He shut the cabinet door and looked at her. "Angela, look, I'm sorry about what happened with the girls. I was pretty sure I had a handle on things. Pretty sure I had things under control, and then—"

"Michael." She went to him, laying her hands on his chest—wanting, needing to touch him. "You did a wonderful job."

"Yeah?" His face brightened at her words and her closeness.

"Yeah." She smiled. "I couldn't have done it better myself."

"How much did you hear?"

"Enough to know that the girls were probably having one of their world-class arguments." She shrugged. "Kids fight, Michael. It's part of life and growing up and having friends. But the important thing is that they fight fair and that they make up afterward and not do anything deliberately to hurt one another, and if they do, that they apologize and make things right. I think that's something you taught Emma today in a way that she'll remember. I'm very grateful for that."

"Yeah?" he said again, pleased.

"Yeah." Unable to resist, Angela stood on tiptoe and brushed her lips against his.

His hands slid to her waist and he drew her close, savoring the taste and feel of her. His body immediately responded, and he drew her closer still, taking the kiss deeper until she moaned softly, lifting her arms to his neck and swaying against him.

The world tilted. Right under her feet in her own kitchen. At least that's the way it felt to Angela as Michael's warmth seemed to seep into her, satisfying some ancient, primal longing that until this moment, she'd been unaware of.

Moaning softly, she swayed against him until she could feel his masculine hardness pressed firmly against her softness, making her ache and yearn for him.

She fit in his arms perfectly, he thought, as if she had been made for him. With his eyes closed and his arms filled with her, Michael realized he was losing himself in her sweet, feminine touch, her taste, her arms. He found the hunger for her growing like an insidious inferno, leaping into his heart, his mind, his soul until he felt as if he would go mad with longing. For her. Only for her.

She was everything he'd ever wanted, needed, desired. Everything he'd denied himself for so very long. Now he couldn't even remember why. It didn't matter. Nothing mattered but the woman in his arms and the feelings swamping him.

When his tongue snaked out and touched hers, she sighed, the sound coming from deep within her as her heart thundered madly until she was certain it would thunder right out of her chest.

Moaning softly, Angela tightened her arms around Michael, clinging to him, fearing her legs would buckle if she didn't. Never had she felt anything this strong, this powerful. Never before had a kiss simply shattered every sane thought until she was left a quivering mass of feelings, needs and desires that she'd never known existed.

Trembling, Angela savored the moment and the man, knowing that she was playing with fire and was getting dangerously close to getting burned. She knew she should stop, knew it in her heart and in her mind, but she couldn't seem to drag her mouth from his, couldn't seem to break the bond that seemed to be drawing her closer to him day by day, hour by hour, as surely as if they'd been tethered together.

Something about Michael touched her in ways that no one ever had before, and she found that she had no defense against him—not against his kindness, his gentleness, his goodness. He was all the things she'd always wanted and needed, all the things she knew she could never have.

"Michael." Reluctantly, she pulled back and away from him, clinging to the front of his shirt until she was certain her legs were steady enough to hold her. Her entire body was vibrating with need. "I'm sorry. I didn't—"

"No." He pressed a finger to her lips, which were still red and a bit swollen from his. "Don't say you're sorry. Please."

The look in his eyes, the tone of his voice, caused her to swallow her words. No, she wasn't sorry, she realized. Not sorry at all. And she wasn't ever going to lie to him again. She didn't regret the kiss; in fact, she wanted more. And was heartily ashamed of her want.

"Okay. I won't say I'm sorry." Her voice was shakier than she would have liked, but it couldn't be helped. She was shakier than she would have liked.

"Good." He touched her face. "Because I'm not, Angela. Not sorry at all."

She nodded, still standing so close to him she could feel the warmth of his body warm her. If she didn't step back or move away from him she was going to do something foolish, something she'd no doubt regret. So reluctantly, she stepped back, giving herself a mental shake to clear her head. Clearing her heart wouldn't be quite so easy, especially since she'd feared that Michael had buried himself there, deep and well, so that getting him out might be an impossibility.

The thought caused a shiver to shudder over her and Angela absently rubbed her hands up and down her arms. "As I was saying, Michael." She dared a glance at him. "I really appreciate you watching the girls and teaching them such a valuable lesson."

"Well, I can't take all the credit. I did have some help."

"Help?" she asked, confused. "What kind of help?"

"My sister, Maggy. I called her this morning just to be certain I could handle this babysitting thing."

"Your sister, Maggy?" Angela frowned. "But Michael, I thought you said your sister Maggy doesn't have any children yet. That she's expecting her first child in a few months?"

"She is. Twins. But she's sort of an expert on advice. Ever read Aunt Millie's column?"

"You mean the advice columnist?"

"That's the one."

"I read Aunt Millie's column every day. But what does your sister have to do with Aunt Millie's column?"

"My sister is Aunt Millie."

She stared at him for a moment. "Your sister is Aunt Millie? The advice columnist?"

"One and the same."

Angela shook her head. "Wait a minute. Your sister's famous and you never thought to mention it?"

He shrugged, trying not to grin at the look on her face. "I didn't think it was important. She's only been Aunt Millie for about a year and it's hard to think of Maggy as famous. It's a long story, but she took over the column from her husband's grandmother, the real Aunt Millie. Millicent Gibson, who, by the way is now married to my grandfather. Anyway—"

Angela held up her hand. "You lost me somewhere along the line, Michael. Back up a bit and explain."

"Millicent Gibson was the original Aunt Millie. She wanted to retire, and my grandfather, who had known Millicent forty years ago, renewed their friendship and suggested my sister, Maggy, would be perfect to take over her column upon her retirement. Well, Millicent's grandson, Griffin, who is now married to Maggy, didn't take too kindly to either my grandfather or my sister—at first. But then he fell in love with Maggy and married her. And my grandfather married Millicent, who retired, and Maggy took over the Aunt Millie column, thus making my sister Aunt Millie. Is that clearer now?"

"Yeah. Clearer, but unbelievable." Cocking her head, Angela studied him for a moment. "Do you have any other famous relatives I should know about?"

"Not unless you count my brother, Finn."

"You have a brother named Finn?"

Michael grinned. "Yeah, and a brother named Patrick, and Collin, and then there's the twins, Tyler and Trace." Michael frowned. "Wait, I'm forgetting someone." He thought for a moment. "No, if you count Finn that's everyone."

"Okay, so why is your brother Finn famous?"

"Infamous might be more like it."

Angela laughed. "Okay, I'll bite. Why's Finn infamous?"

"Well, do you remember me telling you about my

grandfather being able to give Em a run for her matchmaking money?"

"Yeah."

"Well, my grandfather is also a master at stirring up trouble, especially for his grandchildren. Finn's just finishing up law school, and while he's in school, he's been working for the city of Chicago." As a cop, he thought, but didn't add. "And in case you haven't heard, the mayor of the city of Chicago is from one of the most prominent political families in the country."

"So I've heard," Angela said with a smile. Everyone in the country knew about Chicago's infamous politics and political families.

"Anyway, one day my grandfather got annoyed at the mayor for something, and decided that the man had gotten too big for his britches. So he and his cronies got together and put together a write-in campaign for a new candidate for mayor."

"Oh, my, not Finn?" Angela asked, trying to suppress a grin.

"Oh, yeah, Finn. And considering the mayor is Finn's boss, along with just about everyone else in my family, let's just say neither Finn nor the mayor were pleased with my grandfather and his cronies."

Angela chuckled. "I think your grandfather just might have Emma beat."

"I'll second that," he said with a smile. "Now what about you, Angela, what about your family?"

"There's no one left but me and Uncle Jimmy—my parents passed away shortly after my twentieth birthday. That's why when he had his first heart attack six years ago, I came out to help him with the inn."

Michael frowned. Something didn't add up. "Six years ago?" he repeated and she nodded. "Emma must have been a newborn then."

"She wasn't even born yet." At Michael's surprised look, Angela shrugged, then went on. "I was actually in the beginning of my ninth month of pregnancy when Uncle Jimmy had his first heart attack. He's the only family I had left, and I knew he'd need some help with the inn and with his recovery, so I came out to see what I could do."

"Nine months' pregnant?" he repeated, stunned.

"Yep."

"And you never left?" he asked.

"No. I found that I not only loved the peace and quiet here, Michael, but I thought it was a perfect place to raise a child."

"What about Emma's father, Angela?" he asked quietly, his gaze steady on hers.

"What about him?" Angela repeated, stiffening a bit. She hadn't intended for this conversation to turn personal. She never discussed her personal life with anyone, especially her guests. But Michael had become so much more than a guest.

"Surely he must have had a say in you moving here to take a job running an inn while you were pregnant and about to give birth to his child?"

"No, actually, he didn't." Lifting her chin, she forced herself to meet Michael's gaze. "By that time, Michael, I was divorced from Emma's father."

"I see," he said quietly. Angela looked so small, so fragile and so incredibly vulnerable all of a sudden, with her eyes as wide and luminous like a deer caught in headlights; he simply wanted to wrap his arms around her and hold her close, to protect her from whatever had put that awful pain in her eyes and her voice.

Someone had hurt her badly and her fear, wariness and suspicions were apparently just a reaction to that.

"Does Emma's father ever see her?" he asked quietly, realizing not once since he'd arrived at the inn had Emma ever mentioned her father.

"No, he doesn't, Michael. He's never seen her," Angela said.

"Never seen her?" he repeated, shocked. He merely stared at Angela for a moment, unable to grasp the fact that a father would never have seen his own child. "I'm sorry, Angela, that's not a concept I can even conceive, let alone understand. How can a man not see his own child?" He shook his head. "I guess because in my family, well, family is sacrosanct, especially a child. I mean, to be blessed with such a precious gift and then to simply walk away from that gift—that child—is almost blasphemous as far as I'm concerned."

Charmed and touched more than she could ever reveal by his words in defense of Emma, Angela smiled, trying to keep a tight rein on her heart, as well as her emotions.

He stirred something inside of her, something deep and dark. It scared her and left her feeling open and vulnerable, something she hadn't felt in a very long time. If she didn't know better, she'd swear she was falling in love with him; but that, she knew was an impossibility, something she could never allow.

"Not everyone feels that way, Michael," she said softly.

"I know, but can you at least tell me why? I mean why on earth hasn't Emma's father ever seen her?" His temper was carefully controlled, but at the moment he feared it might flare up. He couldn't remember the last time he'd felt his temper jump to a boil so quickly, but the inequity and downright cruelty of what she was telling him went against everything he'd ever believed in when it came to family.

"Emma's a girl."

"A girl? Yeah, so…" He shrugged, totally lost. "Emma's a girl, so what does that have to do with anything?"

"He wanted a boy."

"A boy," Michael repeated, still not certain he was getting this. "So are you telling me that because Emma's a girl her father…what? Isn't interested in her? Doesn't want her? Doesn't see her?"

"Actually, all of the above," Angela confirmed quietly, refusing to lie about the situation.

"But she's his child," Michael said unnecessarily, his own anger and frustration seeping into his words and making her smile. "How on earth could he just walk away from her?"

"He didn't, Michael," Angela said quietly. "I walked away from him."

Michael's eyes narrowed on her beautiful face. "Because you knew he would reject Emma because she was a female?" No wonder the kid was trying to find a husband for her mother. And a father for herself, Michael thought. She'd never had one. He felt his heart soften even more toward Emma. She was a beautiful, special child who deserved to be loved and wanted.

"No." Angela's chin lifted stubbornly and her dark eyes flashed for a moment. "Because he'd lied to me and deceived me about who and what he was from the moment I met him." She shrugged. "His father was a small-time criminal who was building a small, criminal empire with his son's help. I thought he owned a small trucking firm until I learned he used those trucks to transport stolen goods. When I did, when I realized that the man I'd married, the man I thought I had been in love with and built a life with and had a future with, had been lying to me from day one, not only about who he was, but what he did—what his family did," she corrected, blowing out another breath, "I was devastated."

He could see the devastation still, the hurt in her eyes and her face. Hear it in her words. Now he understood so much more about her. The wariness and fear she always wore like a second skin whenever he got too close. To watch her face, to hear her tell him the truth about Emma's birth and her life made him understand so much more about her.

And why she reacted to him the way she did. Something soft, warm and totally protective curled around his heart, making him want to reach out and hold her—and Em—close to comfort and protect them so no one could hurt them again.

"Angela, I'm sorry," he said, touching her cheek. "I'm so very sorry."

"Thank you, Michael," she said quietly, blinking back tears. "But there's nothing to be sorry for. When I found out the truth about my husband, about who he really was— the protégé son of a small time mafia kingpin, I immediately filed for divorce. I didn't even know his real name," she said in disbelief, still unable to believe her own stupidity after all these years. Blinking hard, she wouldn't allow the tears to form. She was beyond that now, way beyond it. The shock and pain at her own naïveté had eased to a dull ache, so that now, all that was left was a lingering sadness for herself and especially for Emma.

"I couldn't be married to a man who'd deliberately deceived me about everything, including who he really was." She hesitated, taking a breath and wearily laying a hand on Michael's chest in an action that was so comforting, so natural, she wasn't even aware of it. "It was as if my whole life, my whole marriage was a lie. Can you understand that, Michael? How can someone live a lie?"

"Yeah," he said with a nod, feeling a well of guilt flood him. "I understand completely. No one should have to live like that."

Hadn't he been doing the exact same thing?

Lying to Angela and deceiving her about who he was and what he really did for a living?

He'd been doing it since he'd arrived, he realized.

No, his mind corrected. It wasn't the same. Not nearly the same. He was doing it to protect both Angela and Emma, to protect them from having the press perhaps swoop down on them here, turning their lives and their home into a three-ring circus. Not to mention the danger that might come along with the discovery of who he really was and where he really was.

He'd been working undercover for months, and had put a great many people away during that time, people who would gladly want to harm him or anyone he cared about simply because of his job, and he wouldn't ever jeopardize Angela or Emma that way. Not now, not ever. And if that meant he had to continue to conceal who he really was and why he was here, then so be it.

"We learned Emma was a girl right about the time I learned the truth about him. When he found out I wasn't carrying a son, he didn't care that I wanted a divorce, didn't care about seeing the child. He was an only son and wanted a son to carry on his family name. Since I wasn't about to give him one, he just figured he'd let us go. I didn't care whether I had a boy, a girl or one of each. I only knew that I had to make a safe, secure home for my child, a child who was not going to grow up in a make-believe world surrounded by deception and lies and a father who spent his life deceiving his family, not to mention the law. So I filed for divorce and I was granted full custody of my unborn child since my ex had no interest in Emma, nor did he want any visitation rights. He basically washed his hands of Em before she was even born."

"Jerk," Michael muttered heatedly, causing Angela to smile and lift a hand to his cheek.

"Michael, it really worked out for the best. I've got Emma and have built a wonderful, safe, secure life for her. A life where she knows she's wanted and loved, and to me that's the most important thing a parent can give their child."

"I know, but—"

"It's not fair?" Angela said with a lift of her brow, filling in the words he was about to say. He nodded and she smiled. "No one ever promised life would be fair, Michael. We just do the best we can with the hand we've been dealt. I'm not going to tell you it's been easy, but we've managed."

"Raising a child alone is never easy," he said, thinking of his mother who'd raised Michael and his siblings after their father was killed in the line of duty and then later his grandfather.

"No, it's not. But I've made it work. I think Emma is doing wonderfully. She's happy, secure and, other than trying to pawn me off as a wife to friends, neighbors and any other man she comes across, I think she's relatively normal," Angela added with a small chuckle. "A bit precocious at times, but I just think that's part of her charm."

Michael chuckled. "She's a pistol, Angela. She's warm, loving, kind and trusting. And I think that's a testament to you and the wonderful job you've done with her." He skimmed a hand down her cheek. "She's a terrific kid and any man would be proud and lucky to call her his own."

"Thanks, Michael." She blushed, pleased and embarrassed and rattled more than she believed possible by his words and his touch, not to mention his nearness. "And I agree," she added with a mother's pride, glancing at the kitchen clock. "But I guarantee she's probably also hungry, so I'd better get these groceries put away before the girls come down wanting their snack."

"I'll help," Michael said.

"Michael, you don't have to help. You've done more than enough for one day."

"On the contrary, Angela, I want to help. Teamwork seems to work best around here."

Angela smiled at him. She'd never considered the concept that she could be part of a team, part of a couple who did things together *as* a team. She'd never had the luxury of having a partner before, but having Michael here helping had given her an idea of just how wonderful it could be. "Yes, it does, Michael," she said with a smile, wondering just for a moment what it would be like to have Michael as her partner in life, as well. She quickly banished the thought before it could take hold. "Michael, you never told me what advice your sister Maggy gave you for watching the girls."

He chuckled. "She told me no matter what happens, never let them see my fear."

Angela smiled. That might be good advice for any woman dealing with a man, as well.

Chapter Six

During the next week Mother Nature cooperated, Emma went back to school, Michael spent most of his days out in the shed scraping paint off the patio furniture and prepping it for a new coat of paint, and Angela kept her promise to herself to get an early start on baking her cookies for the Christmas festival.

Since Emma had a Brownie meeting the following Saturday and was assigned to bring treats, Angela decided to bake several dozen extra cookies for Emma to take to her meeting. Angela was just finishing the icing on the last batch when someone knocked at the back door, startling her and the dogs, who'd been comfortably snoozing there.

"It's okay, boys," she soothed, grabbing a dish towel to wipe her hands as she headed toward the back door. She knew it wasn't Michael; he had been going in and out of the house all week and hadn't bothered to knock. Angela opened the door after nudging the growling dogs out of the way.

"Hi, Ms. DiRosa." Swallowing heavily, eighteen-year-old Andy Jr. from the garage in town shyly glanced at her from under the brim of his bright red cap advertising his dad's garage.

"Hi, Andy." Smiling, she motioned him inside. "Come on in out of the cold." She held the door open for him as he snatched his cap off his head, leaving his wispy golden blond hair all but standing up on end.

"I was just finishing some cookies. Would you like some?"

"Yes, ma'am. Thank you," he said, leaning down to pet the dogs.

"How's your father, Andy?" Angela asked, as she poured him a glass of milk and placed some still-warm cookies on a plate at the table.

"Fine, ma'am. Daddy's just fine. Working hard as ever, though," Andy Jr. said.

"I'll bet he's been real busy with these storms."

"Yes, ma'am," Andy Jr. said, sitting when she pulled out a chair for him and gestured him into it. "There've been a whole lotta accidents since the first storm and a lot of dead batteries and frozen gas lines. Lots of fender benders, too," he added, setting his cap on the table and taking a cookie from the plate she offered. "But you know how people are about their vehicles. They need them to be in top running condition in this kind of winter."

"I know," Angela said. "The inn's van's about due for servicing. I'm hoping to get it in sometime next week."

"Say, Angela," Michael said, pushing open the back door and stepping into the kitchen without glancing up.

"Have you got any more turpentine?" Michael glanced up, saw the young boy sitting at the table and smiled as he stomped his feet on the carpet at the back door. "Hi, there."

"Sir." Andy Jr. bolted up from his chair as if he'd been shot from a cannon. "It's nice to meet you, sir."

"It's Michael," he said with a smile, moving toward the table and Andy and extending his hand. "The only person who calls me sir is my lawyer."

"Yes, sir," Andy Jr. said, shaking Michael's hand and blushing. "I mean, Michael."

"Michael's a guest here at the inn," Angela clarified, knowing how quickly rumors and gossip spread in a small town like Chester Lake. As a single mom, the last thing she needed was someone gossiping about her. "In fact, it's his car I called your dad about and asked him to have a look at."

Andy Jr.'s eyes widened as his gaze jumped to Michael's. He all but sank down in his chair again. "Sir, is that your vintage '67 Mustang we towed in?" he asked, his eyes going bright and dreamy.

"It's mine," Michael confirmed, reaching for a cookie and pulling a chair out to sit down.

"Wow, it sure is a beauty." Andy Jr. shook his head. "I've been doing the work on it, and I gotta tell you, she sure is a beauty. I haven't seen one in that good a shape in a long, long time. Maybe never."

"My brother, Patrick, is a vintage car buff. Restoring vintage cars is kind of a hobby of his." Michael took a big bite of his cookie. "He's the one who found the Mustang for me, and he's the one who takes care of it, and Patrick's pretty particular. Actually, he's fussy," Michael confessed with a laugh, "about his 'babies' as he calls them." Cocking his head, Michael studied the kid. He had a feeling the kid was as big of a car buff as his brother Patrick. "He's got a '62 'Vette he's been restoring for the past year. When he's finished, he's going to sell it, so if you know anyone who might be interested, I think I could get them a good deal."

"Wow. Really?" Forgetting himself, Andy all but bounced in his chair. "I'd just about die to own a 'Vette. I've worked on them most of my life, and I gotta tell you they are some sweet, mean machines." He laughed. "And they can go like the wind."

"Tell you what, Andy. Next time I talk to my brother, I'll ask him how close he is to finishing and what kind of money he's looking for." Michael shrugged, remembering the days when he was eighteen and only wanted a hot car and an even hotter girl. He glanced at Angela and almost smiled. Well, some things never changed.

"That would be mag, sir," Andy Jr. said with a grin, forgetting himself and reaching for another cookie. "Totally mag." He took a bite and then frowned, remembering why he was here. "Oh, I almost forgot. Your car should be ready by Friday. I'm just waiting for a part to come in from Green Bay. Should be here late this afternoon. So tomorrow morning, I'll get it installed, and it should be ready to pick up sometime before closing tomorrow."

"Sounds great," Michael said. "Know what the damages are?"

"Sorry." Andy Jr. shook his head. "My ma handles the books." He grinned sheepishly. "My dad and I, well, as my ma says, she doesn't stick her nose under our hoods, and we're not allowed to stick our noses in her books." Andy grinned. "She'll give you the damages when you pick up the car."

"Fair enough."

"Would you like some more cookies, Andy?" Angela asked, making him shake his head.

"No, ma'am. I've got to be going." Realizing he hadn't touched his milk, Andy Jr. grabbed the glass and downed it in one gulp. "I've got to be going. I was out this way to pick up a tow so I thought I'd just stop by and give you an update on the Mustang." He stood up, grabbing his cap off the table and settling it on his head. "Oh, Ms. DiRosa?"

"Yes, Andy?"

"Could you, uh, tell Emma something for me?"

"Sure," Angela said.

"Last time you were at the garage, Emma asked me if I liked kids and if I wanted any. I didn't get a chance to answer her, so could you tell her for me that I guess I like kids." He shrugged. "I'm a bit too young to be thinking about a family and all, seeing's how I still haven't finished school, but I guess I like kids as well as the next guy."

"Kids?" Angela repeated in disbelief, trying not to blush.

"Yeah." Andy Jr. lifted his cap to scratch his wispy head of hair. "I don't know why she was asking, but I thought it might have been important to her."

Angela wanted to groan. Her daughter was matchmaking again. This time with a boy not even old enough to shave, let alone vote. What on earth was she going to do with that child?

"I'll tell her," Angela said, not daring to look at Michael.

"Nice meeting you, sir," Andy Jr. said, extending his hand to Michael. "I'll be mighty appreciative if you'd let me know about that car."

"Will do," Michael promised, trying to contain his grin. Apparently Emma had moved on to the next candidate in her search for a father. He probably wouldn't have found it so amusing if Angela hadn't been quite so embarrassed.

"Tell your father I said hi and thank you, Andy," Angela said as she opened the back door for him.

"Will do, Ms. DiRosa. Thanks for the cookies and milk."

"You're welcome," Angela said as she watched him walk down the drive. She shut the door quietly, then turned to Michael. "Don't say it," she warned, lifting her hand in the air. "Just don't even say it."

"What? What?" he asked innocently, trying not to grin as he leaned against the counter and crossed his arms across his chest.

"Don't say a word about Emma's matchmaking." Angela cleared the table, setting the dirty plate and glass in the sink, wishing she didn't suddenly feel so exposed and vulnerable. "Honestly, Michael, what on earth am I going to do with that child?"

"Well, it seems to me that Emma's trying to tell you something," he said mildly.

"Tell me something?" she repeated blankly.

He nodded. "Seems to me she's trying to tell you that she wants and needs a father, and that you need a husband."

"I…I…I…" At a total loss as to what to say, especially since he looked so smug about it, Angela had the urge to simply throw something. "That's ridiculous," she snapped. "I need a husband like…like…a goldfish needs a bow tie. And as for a father, Emma had a father, Michael, and remember how well that turned out?" She hated the bitterness in her voice, but she simply couldn't help it.

"Yeah, I remember, but do you remember the old saying?"

"What old saying?" she snapped crossly.

"If at first you don't succeed…" He leaned over and

kissed her, quickly pulling back before she could object, but not before he saw the desire—and the longing—flash in her eyes. "Try, try again," he whispered, leaning his brow against hers and hating the sadness and regret he saw flicker through her eyes.

"I don't know that I can try again, Michael," she admitted honestly, wanting nothing more than to throw her arms around him and burrow her head into his shoulder and bury her past and all the pain and humiliation with it. "I don't know if I can ever trust anyone that much again. It involves a great deal of risk, not just for myself, but for Emma, as well," she said quietly, knowing what he was asking. "And I don't know if I'm willing to take that risk."

Nodding quietly, Michael brushed his lips against hers. "Well, at least it's something to think about and consider. Big risks, big rewards, Angela. Think about it." He kissed her again quickly, then turned and let himself out the back door, whistling softly.

Big risks, big rewards. The words reverberated in Angela's mind, making her realize just how big a risk would be required to totally trust Michael.

In the past few days, it had been very hard to come to terms with her feelings for Michael. It was no use denying she *had* feelings, because then she'd simply be lying to herself, something she simply couldn't do. It just wasn't her style not to face things honestly and then deal with them.

But how was she supposed to deal with her feelings?

She hadn't a clue.

Perhaps because it had been so long since she'd *had* any feelings like this—romantic feelings that only served to fuel the longing and yearnings she thought she'd buried years ago.

She had to admit she'd been thinking about what it would be like to have Michael in her life, as her husband, as Emma's father, as her partner—forever. Faced with the reality that she was still capable of feeling that way about someone, since she'd spent so much time with him—day in, day out, working together side-by-side, spending every evening together—she knew she couldn't deny what was in her heart.

Or on her mind. The thought of having a permanent relationship with Michael was both thrilling and terrifying. Trusting someone that much, trusting him with her heart and her daughter's fragile heart, well, now that would require the amount and kind of trust she wasn't sure she was willing to give to anyone, not even to Michael.

And then, of course, there was the reality of their situation.

Michael would be leaving soon, she knew. She knew that he would go back to his home, his family and his life in Chicago, back to where he came from.

And where, she wondered, would that leave her and Emma? It would leave them both with hurt feelings and possibly broken hearts. Something she swore she'd never allow to happen.

Realizing just how far she'd allowed her romantic dreams to develop made her suddenly furious with herself. Not so much for her sake—she was an adult and could accept adult disappointments and realities—but what about Emma?

Had she allowed Emma to have false hope that Michael would become a permanent part of their lives when she had absolutely no right to allow Emma to even consider such a thing?

She had no idea how Michael felt about her or Emma. Oh, sure, he lavished time and attention on Emma, but that certainly was not the same as assuming the day-to-day responsibilities of parenting a child. That would require major love and commitment, something Michael had never hinted at or mentioned. He'd never given her reason to hope or have such foolish daydreams. And a few stolen kisses hardly amounted to any kind of commitment, she realized dully.

Grabbing a sponge, Angela began to scrub down the already clean counter with more force than necessary, knowing she should have put a stop to this—this closeness between Emma and Michael—sooner, rather than later. She had just been going along, assuming the days would take care of themselves, when in fact, she should have seen just how attached Emma had become to Michael.

Emma was just a little girl, a little girl who apparently was desperately in need of some male attention, affection, acceptance and love.

Emma had begun to expect Michael to be there every day, had come to expect that Michael would just be a part of their lives.

But it was only temporary, Angela realized, scrubbing the counter harder. Michael was leaving and where would that leave her precious daughter?

Angela shook her head, feeling a sick sense of dread curl in her stomach. Emma was going to get hurt; there was no getting around it. Not this time. Emma was far too attached emotionally to Michael, and Angela should never have let things get this far.

How, Angela wondered, had Michael gotten under their skins and into their hearts so easily?

She wasn't quite sure. But now that it had happened, she had to correct the situation before Emma got attached any further to Michael.

She was simply going to have to talk to Emma, to tell her—remind her—that Michael wasn't going to be here forever. That Michael wasn't a permanent part of their lives. That Michael would be leaving soon, and leaving them behind.

In less than two weeks, at the end of the Christmas festival, Michael's month-long vacation would be over and it would be time for him to leave. And Angela and Emma were just going to have to deal with it.

Shaking her head, Angela wondered how on earth she was going to remind her daughter of that—without breaking her heart.

She didn't know, but she knew she'd better figure it out—soon.

"Mama, Mama, guess what? Guess what? Guess *what!*" Emma said, barreling through the back door, slamming it shut soundly behind her. "Mama!"

"I'm right here, honey," Angela said, pushing through the door into the kitchen. "Stay right there, Em," she scolded. "And take your coat and boots off before you track snow and water all through the house."

"But Mama, I gotta tell you what happened at school today." The papers clutched in Emma's fist waved wildly in the air. "I got a gold star on my story, the one Michael helped me write. I'm the only one who got a gold star in the whole class and it's 'cuz of Michael." Emma continued to bounce, spraying snow and melting ice over the floor. "Where is he, mama? I have to tell him. I have to tell him."

"He's upstairs working," Angela said, unwinding the woolen scarf from around Emma's neck and taking the papers from her hand before she crumpled them further. "And you know we're not supposed to bother him when he's working."

"Is he writing, Mama?" Emma asked, plopping down on the floor so her mother could pry off her bright yellow snow boots.

"Yes, sweetheart, he's writing." Angela dropped her daughter's snow boots to the plastic floor mat and then lifted Emma's chin, sorry to deflate her enthusiasm, but knowing Michael needed this time. "Do you think you can wait until he comes down for dinner to tell him your news?"

Emma nodded, biting the end of her mittens to pull them off with her teeth. "Okay," she said glumly. "I could wait."

"That's a good girl," Angela beamed at her, unzipping her daughter's heavy down coat and slipping it off of her. "But how about if I read your story in the meantime?"

"You can't!" Emma said quickly and then blushed guiltily. "I mean, it's a surprise, Mama. A big surprise." Emma's eyes danced in excitement. "It's part of your Christmas present, and Michael helped me with it, but you gotta wait 'til Christmas to read it." Emma hesitated, looking for her papers again. "Is that okay, Mama?"

Now Michael was helping Emma with Christmas. Goodness, this had gone further than she'd expected, with Emma getting more attached than she'd anticipated. "It's fine, sweetheart. Just fine. You go on upstairs and get changed and put your story away. Then come back down and you can have a snack. But don't bother Michael, promise?"

"I promise," Emma said glumly, then brightened suddenly. "Barbie asked me to come over and play until dinner. Can I go, Mama, huh, please?"

Angela thought for a moment, glancing at the oven where dinner was already cooking. She supposed she could wait a few more hours to have that talk with Emma. She really was in no hurry to break her daughter's heart. "Sure, honey. Go on up and change, and when you come down, I'll walk you over."

Angela was just finishing setting the dinner table when Michael came back downstairs. "Something smells wonderful," he said, letting the kitchen door swing shut behind him.

"It's stuffed peppers with mashed potatoes and tomato gravy," Angela said with a smile, glancing up at him from the last place setting she put in place.

"Where's Em?" Michael asked, glancing around. "It's been way too quiet around here this afternoon."

"She's over at Barbie's playing." Angela glanced at the clock. "In fact, I've got to go over and get her right now. Dinner's almost ready." She untied the apron she had on over her sweatpants and hung it on the hook by the back door.

"Let me go, Angela," Michael offered. "I need a bit of fresh air to clear my head."

"Problems?" Angela asked, looking at him carefully. He shook his head.

"No, not really." He hesitated before going to the coat rack and plucking his leather jacket up. "I've finished the first half of the book." It had gone surprisingly quickly, and well, he thought. The characters seemed to have taken on a life of their own. He'd had the basic outline of the story plotted out, but the individual scenes, the tone and everything else just sort of took off once he started writing. It was both surprising and startling to him.

He hated to admit that it had gone so well that he couldn't wait to get back to it. Writing, he'd discovered, had soothed and satisfied something primal and instinctive inside of him, something that made him feel complete for the very first time in his life.

He glanced at Angela again, felt his heart stir and wondered if writing was the only reason he felt so at peace and complete.

"Michael, that's wonderful." Angela knew how hard he'd been working, knew he'd been burning the candle at both ends, doing, really, the work of two full-time jobs. Spending his days doing work for her around the inn, then spending his evenings and nights writing. He was putting in close to eighteen hours a day most days, and she had to admit, she admired his dedication.

"Yeah, I suppose so," he confessed, zipping his jacket up. "But I won't know if it's good or not until someone else reads it."

"Is that an invitation? Because I already told you I'd love to read it, Michael," she said, leaning against the counter and crossing her arms across her breasts.

"I know." He grinned. "I just printed out a copy for you. I left it on the table in the living room." He shrugged, trying not to show how anxious he was. "I thought maybe after dinner if you had time…" He let his words trail off and she nodded.

"I'll get to it as soon as I get the dishes done and Emma tucked into bed for the night."

"Great." Michael reached for the doorknob. "I'll go get Emma." He hesitated. "Angela?"

"Yes, Michael."

"Just tell me honestly what you think. If it's no good, say so."

"I will, Michael," she said carefully. "Promise."

Angela rarely made promises she couldn't keep, and she knew by the end of the first chapter that Michael had something very, very special.

With Emma and her uncle Jimmy already tucked in for the night, she'd taken the dogs out one last time, then curled up on the couch in front of the roaring fire, prepared to do something she hadn't done in a very long time—simply take some time for herself to read and relax with a book.

Reading had always been a lifelong passion, but during the years at the inn, she was always so busy, she rarely had time to indulge in something as simple as curling up with a good book.

By the end of the third chapter, she had the afghan wrapped around her, not because she was particularly cold, but because Michael's book had all but given her the shivers. It was written as all good books were—giving her the feeling she was right there, actually part of the action.

It was a mystery, but one that had so many twists and turns and unexpected side jaunts she found her nerves all but squealing from tenseness.

The manuscript pages seem to fly out of her hands; she couldn't seem to turn them fast enough as she fell wildly, hopelessly in love with the main character—a hard-bitten cop who'd closed himself off from life in order to do his job, who had become bitter and burned-out with the frustration of dealing with the system, and yet was compelled to keep plugging away out of a sense of duty to his late father, a cop who'd been killed in the line of duty by the bad guys.

Now, almost twenty years later, the hero finally had a lead on his father's killers and had set a trap that was both brilliant and diabolical. Yet the hero was fighting his own personal demons of loneliness and isolation.

And that's where the story ended. Frustrated by not knowing what was going to happen, Angela yawned and then stretched, realizing she'd been reading for almost three hours.

After gathering up the loose manuscript pages, Angela headed upstairs, hoping Michael was still awake. The light was on under his door and she knocked gently.

"Michael?" She kept her voice low, and the manuscript gripped tightly in her hands.

He pulled open the door, looking tired and rumpled. She glanced over his shoulder and could see he was still at it.

"I'm finished," she said, handing him back the manuscript.

"And?" Michael said, trying not to let his nerves show as he dropped the loose manuscript pages to the desk.

"It's wonderful, Michael," she said, grinning hugely at him. "Just wonderful. I couldn't put it down and read it all in one sitting. But I've got to tell you, you can't just leave me hanging here. You have to tell me what happens."

He grinned, dragging a hand through his hair and then rubbing the stubble along his chin. He felt like he had sand in his eyes; they were so sore from looking at his computer screen.

"Now Angela," he said, taking her hand and pulling her deeper into the room. "If I tell you how it ends, then you won't want to read the rest of the book."

"On the contrary," she said with a laugh, realizing this was the first time she'd been in his room since the morning after he'd arrived. "I can't wait to read the rest. How long will it take you to finish?"

He shrugged. "I don't know," he answered honestly. And he really didn't. It was difficult to tell how quickly he would be able to finish. The beginning had all but poured out of him, as if he were purging himself. But that didn't necessarily mean that the ending would come as smoothly.

Since this was his first attempt at writing a book, he had no idea how long the rest would take.

"I figure probably another couple of weeks or so with revisions." His brows drew together. "I'm going to try to finish it in two weeks, though."

She nodded, thinking. "Then what happens, Michael?"

"What do you mean?"

"What happens after you finish? Are you going to try to publish it?"

He nodded, then smiled. "Griffin, my brother-in-law, offered to take a look at my book when I'm done." Michael shrugged, trying not to let his excitement show. "He said if it's any good, he'll represent me. He's not just an attorney, but he's also been his grandmother's literary agent for years, as well."

"He's going to try to sell your book," she said hopefully.

"Yeah." Pressing his fingertips to his eyes, Michael stifled another yawn. "I have to finish the book, though. He can't sell it until it's finished."

"Yeah, but Michael, can't you send him the first half so he can at least read it?"

Michael thought about it for a moment. "Yeah, I suppose I could do that, although I hadn't really thought about it."

"I think you should. Think about it." She glanced at the manuscript he'd set down on the bed. "It's really wonderful, Michael, and I'm not just saying that because I don't want to hurt your feelings. It really *is* wonderful." She lifted a hand and touched his cheek. "You are a terrific writer." She laughed suddenly. "Although you did have me almost coming out of my seat a few times." She shook her head. "The cop in there is so realistic, so believable it's almost as if you've lived his life."

He hoped he didn't blush; he hoped he hadn't given himself away. He couldn't tell her, not yet, that he had lived the life of the cop in his book, simply because the cop was *him.* Almost everything in the book was based on incidents from his ten years on the force. And he'd poured a lot of his own personal frustrations into the words, the pages.

Although the bad guys were a composite of a lot of bad guys he'd known and dealt with, everything else was based on his own experiences.

And that, he realized, was what had been bothering him for days. He'd been fighting an internal battle with himself, trying to figure out how the heck he was going to tell Angela the truth about who he was and why he was here.

He still hadn't figured out a solution, but with only two weeks of his vacation left, he knew he was going to have to tell her the truth—and soon.

His feelings for her and for Emma were far too strong for him to ignore or, more importantly, to walk away from. But he couldn't begin to allow himself to think about the future until he'd told Angela the truth about who he was and until he was ready to come to terms with his own personal demons.

And until he figured things out, he couldn't tell Angela

the truth, fearing that she'd turn him away for lying to her and deceiving her, deliberately, just as her husband had done. And he couldn't even bear the thought of possibly losing her and Emma. He just couldn't handle the thought, and so for now, he realized, he'd just have to let things be.

He'd tell her the truth sooner, rather than later, he mused, but on his own terms, terms that included something to offer them. As it was right now, he had nothing to offer Angela and Emma, nothing at all, not considering his own promise to himself.

He cared way too much for Angela and Emma to even consider possibly putting them through what he and his brothers and sister had gone through when their father had been killed. That wasn't something he would ever willingly do to someone he cared about; it wasn't even an option.

So far now, he'd say nothing to her, and figure all of this out in his own time, taking his time to think everything through thoroughly.

"Thanks, Angela, that's quite a compliment."

"Well it's nothing less than the truth." Angela hesitated, glancing out the window across the room at the full moon that hung high and bright in the darkened night sky. "Michael," she began carefully. "Have you given any thought to what you're going to do at the end of your vacation?" She shrugged. "I mean, I know you have to go home. You have a life, a family and a job back in Chicago, but I was just…wondering…" She let her voice trail off, trying to ignore the fluttering of hope in her heart.

"You're worried about Emma," he said, knowing instinctively what was troubling her. Probably because it had been troubling him, as well. The mere thought of leaving Angela and Emma behind, of leaving the peace and tranquility he'd found with them here at the inn, seemed almost inconceivable right now. He'd gotten so used to having them in his life every day—to seeing them, to expecting them to be a part of his life. Maybe it was because they'd become so much a part of his heart.

"Yeah," she admitted, chewing her lower lip. "Em's gotten awfully attached to you, Michael, and I don't think she really realizes that in a couple weeks you'll be leaving to go home." Each word seemed to slice at Angela's heart and she silently hoped, prayed he'd say something—anything to give her some indication that he'd thought about staying. Permanently.

"I know." He blew out breath, wishing he could say something that would erase the worry from her eyes. But at the moment, he couldn't. Not until he got a few things settled in his own head. "I don't know what to do about it, Angela. I don't want to hurt her. That's the last thing in the world I would ever want to do."

"I know," Angela admitted, seeing the pain in his eyes and lifting a hand to his cheek to soothe him. "But she's going to be hurt, Michael. I think in her mind… I think she thinks that you'll be here forever, and I'm afraid I'm going to have to find a way to make her see reality." She supposed in her own mind, she, too, had hoped that somehow, some way, he'd stay. But now, knowing he hadn't planned on it, and apparently hadn't even thought of it, made her feel incredibly foolish, as well as embarrassed. She'd let her own schoolgirl fantasies get the best of her, allowing her to see a future for them together.

Big risk, he'd said. Big rewards.

But in her experience big risks equaled big hurts. Hadn't she learned that lesson once already, she wondered furiously?

She knew better, and it infuriated her that she'd been just as naive as her daughter. At least her daughter had an excuse—her age. Angela had none. She knew better than to risk her heart or her hope. Knew it and had done it anyway.

"Angela." Concerned, Michael stepped closer, slid his hands to her waist. "I don't want to hurt either of you. I can't tell you how much this time here has meant to me. Or how much you and Emma have come to mean to me."

"I know," Angela said, unable to look at him.

Standing here, hearing him admit that he was indeed going to leave, caused something inside of her to throb, like an old wound that had suddenly been opened and was aching. "We've enjoyed having you here as well, Michael." She managed a smile even though she ached inside. "But I'll just have to handle the situation with Emma as best as possible. I don't think either of us thought she'd ever get this attached to you."

"No," he admitted with a crooked grin. "I didn't expect to get this attached to her, either." Or to you, he thought. He had nothing to offer Angela yet. Nothing at all. And until he did, he knew he was better off keeping quiet.

She nodded, stepping back out of his arms. She needed some time alone, to think and to nurse her wounded heart and her pride. "Well, you've got enough on your mind with the book." Smiling, she pushed her hair back off her face. "Emma's my responsibility, and I'll handle her. So please don't worry about it." She flashed him a smile. "I'll let you get back to work. I'm going to call it a night."

"Angela, wait." He caught her arm, not wanting her to leave like this. Something was terribly wrong and he didn't have a clue what. "Are you okay?"

"I'm fine."

He looked at her face carefully. "Are you sure?"

"Michael." She slipped free of his hand. She was going to have to start withdrawing from him on a personal level, putting their relationship back on a totally professional level. It was the only way to try to protect herself from any further hurt. And she had to start now. "I'm perfectly fine. It's late and I'm a bit tired. That's all."

"You're sure?"

She smiled, easing toward the door, anxious to be out and away from his scrutiny. "Positive. Good night, Michael."

"Good night."

She turned and left him standing in the doorway and staring after her.

One thing was certain, Michael mused with a frown as he closed the door. Angela, he'd discovered, was a terrible liar.

Chapter Seven

Determined to finish his book in the precious little time left of his vacation, Michael all but buried himself in his writing. Now that he had his characters established and his primary goal laid out, he found that he was just as anxious to finish the book as he'd been to start it. If he had thought the second half of the book would go more slowly, he would have been wrong.

He'd called his brother-in-law, Griffin, and told him he'd be sending a copy of the first half of the book to him by courier. Griffin should have received it by the first of the week, and although Michael tried not to think about it, it remained in the back of his mind that perhaps, just perhaps, it really wasn't quite good enough to publish.

During the day, he spent most of the week out in the shed, repainting all five sets of patio furniture because each piece required four different procedures, including sealing, and it took him nearly a full day to complete each one. In the evening, he ate dinner with Angela, Emma and Jimmy, and then raced up to his room to write.

With the Christmas festival less than a week away, there was a great deal more to be done. It was midweek before it dawned on him that Angela and Emma were either too busy to spend much time with him, or deliberately avoiding him.

Disturbed, he was determined to deal with it—as soon as he could take a brief break from the book.

On Thursday, he wrote until nearly three in the morning and then fell into bed, totally exhausted and yet exhilarated. He'd finished. He felt such a sense of accomplishment and fulfillment that he couldn't wait to share those feelings with Angela.

On Friday morning he overslept, allowing himself a couple extra hours to make up for the night before. He pushed through the kitchen doors shortly after noon, hair still damp from his shower and fighting back a yawn.

"Good morning," he said to Angela, who was bent over the kitchen table icing cookies. He loved seeing her first thing in the morning, knowing she'd be there, usually in the kitchen, whipping up some fragrant dish.

"Good morning," she replied without glancing up. "There's a fresh pot of coffee on the stove, and some home-made coffee cake in the bread bin." She glanced up just long enough to push her hair out of her eyes with her elbow, the only thing free at the moment. "I've got to finish decorating these cookies, then start decorating the trees in the guest rooms."

"Where's Jimmy?" Michael asked, glancing around the kitchen. The dogs were snoozing by the back door as usual.

"He went to the butcher in town to pick up our meat order for the festival." Angela stood up, laid down the icing bag and then pressed a hand to her aching back. She'd been bent over the table for almost two hours, trying to finish the last of the cookies.

"Meat order?" Michael replied with a lift of his brow as he took a sip of his coffee. "Sounds like you're preparing for an invasion."

"Just about," she said with a laugh, glancing at him. "I'll be preparing three meals a day for more than twenty-five people every day for the next week, and that requires a special meat order. If you look on the refrigerator, on Emma's calendar, you'll see what's on the menu each day." She glanced up at him again and her heart did a slow tumble. He wore a pullover, bulky fisherman's knit sweater and a pair of faded jeans that had holes at the knees and white wear marks just about everywhere else. His feet were bare, except for his thick warm socks, but still, he radiated that intense masculinity she would always associate with him.

"Haven't seen you much the past week," he commented casually, tempted to sneak one of the freshly iced cookies. As if reading his mind, Angela picked several up and handed them to him.

"We've been extremely busy, Michael," she said coolly. "Our first guests arrive on Sunday afternoon, and after that, it's 'Katie, bar the door,'" she finished with a laugh. "We have reservations for the entire week of the festival. And a backup list of reservations in case anyone cancels."

"Does anyone? Cancel I mean?" he asked biting into one of the cookies.

Angela shook her head. "No one has in years. We have standing reservations from year to year, but once in a while, something comes up and we'll have an opening, but it's not too often. We have people who come here from all over, including some from Chicago."

He nodded, although the information sent a frisson of fear racing through him. But the chances of anyone he knew coming up to little Chester Lake, Wisconsin, were so remote as to be ridiculous.

"So, uh, since you hadn't planned on my being here, using a guest room, are you going to want me to leave?" He hadn't thought about his room until just this moment; now, the prospect of actually having to face leaving made his heart jitter in a way it hadn't since he had been a terrified rookie facing someone with a loaded gun for the first time.

She turned to look at him, surprised to find such concern on his face. "Actually, Michael, that won't be necessary. I know you still have a week left on your vacation, and if you'd like to stay, to continue to work, I could use the help. And I've arranged for Emma to move into my room, and you can take her room. That is, if you don't mind sleeping in a pink-and-white room for a week."

Relieved, he let out a breath he hadn't realized he'd been holding. "No, Angela, I don't mind at all. In fact, I appreciate it. But how is Emma going to feel about it?"

"Emma." Angela blew out a breath. Dealing with her daughter this week had been just short of difficult. She'd had her talk with her daughter earlier in the week, explaining that Michael would be leaving soon, but Emma wasn't having any of it. Her daughter was convinced that Michael was staying, permanently, and wouldn't even consider the possibility that she could be wrong. And Angela still had no idea what to do about it. "Well, let's just say she's glad you'll be here for the festival."

"So am I, Angela," he said quietly, coming up behind her. "So am I." Unable to resist, and realizing he hadn't touched her or been close to her for almost a week, Michael bent and kissed her neck.

For an instant, Angela was tempted to lean into him, then she caught herself and straightened, moving out of his reach just as the phone rang.

"I hope that's not Uncle Jimmy calling to tell me the butcher has screwed up my meat order again," she said, wiping her hands down her apron. "Last year there was nearly mass chaos because none of the fish I ordered came in, and the butcher and Uncle Jimmy nearly came to blows over it." She snatched up the phone, nodding at him when he reached for another cookie.

"Chester Lake Inn," Angela said into the phone. "Yes, hello, Mrs. Ingland." Her face brightened to a smile. "How are you? What?" Her face drained of color as her fingers tightened on the receiver, turning her knuckles white. "Oh, dear God, is she all right?" Fear rose in the back of her throat, almost choking her. "How? When? Yes, yes, I'm on my way. Please, Mrs. Ingland, tell her I'm on my way. Yes, I'll meet you there. Please tell her I'll be right there." With shaking hands, Angela hung up the phone.

"Angela." Michael was at her side in three long strides. "What is it? What's wrong? You're white as a sheet." He clamped his hands down on her shoulders and felt her trembling violently. She lifted her face to his; her eyes were wide and shimmering with tears and fear. Her cheeks had gone white and translucent.

"Emma." She pressed her fingers to her mouth so she wouldn't scream. "It's Emma," she managed finally, her voice as shaky as she was. "She's been hurt, Michael."

"Hurt?" His heart began a jitterbug of fear. "What happened?" he asked, trying to keep his own voice calm. The last thing Angela needed right now was for him to lose his cool.

"She's had an accident."

"What happened?" Shock and fear intermingled in his system, sending adrenaline flooding through his limbs.

"She fell off the monkey bars at school during recess." Angela shook her head, tried to think, tried to clear her mind of the fear, but she couldn't seem to get around it. Emma had never been hurt, never been hospitalized in her life, not since her birth. "The hospital." Angela closed her eyes and took a deep breath, trying to calm herself so she could think. But the fear and panic were so huge that she couldn't do anything but shake. "I have to get to the hospital," she said suddenly. "Keys. I need my car keys." Blindly, she walked around the kitchen as if she'd never seen it before. "They've called an ambulance. I have to meet them at the hospital. Where are my car keys?"

"Angela." Following her, he took her by the shoulders and turned her to him, his heart aching for her and for Emma. "It's okay, Angela. She's going to be fine. Kids fall and get hurt all the time," he said, wishing he felt as confident as his words. He couldn't even imagine, or bear the thought of Emma being hurt or scared. It brought every ounce of love and protectiveness out in him.

Nodding, Angela tried to swallow past the lump in her throat. "I have to go. My keys. I have to find my car keys." She found them in the usual place on the key rack near the back door. Michael deftly lifted them out of her hands.

"Angela, you're in no condition to drive. Let me take you."

She nodded, reaching for her coat. "Please, let's just go," she pleaded, struggling into her coat. "The hospital is past town, about twenty-five minutes away." She glanced at the clock. "We should get there just about the same time as the ambulance."

"Boots." He glanced down at himself. "Wait, I've got to put my boots on." He grabbed them from the plastic snow mat and stuffed his feet into them. "Why don't you write Jimmy a note, telling him where we've gone? Just so he won't worry."

Wringing her hands together and with her coat hanging open, Angela looked at him blankly. Then she suddenly nodded, going back by the telephone to get a notepad and pen.

"Angela?"

She glanced up, tears shimmering in her eyes as her shaky hands composed a brief note.

"Don't worry, I'll be there with you every step of the way, and I promise she'll be fine."

"What in the hell is taking so long?" Michael grumbled as he paced the length of the hospital waiting room. "They've been in there for over an hour." Michael blew out a breath, and glanced at the double doors that separated them from the examining rooms and Emma.

"I don't know." Angela sat on a chair, her coat hanging open, as tears silently ran down her face. A cup of coffee a nurse had brought her sat untouched on the small table bolted down next to her. "I just don't know, Michael." She glanced up at him, clenching her hands together. Her heart seemed to be pumping at twice its normal rate. "I can't believe they won't let me see her." Knowing Emma was just through those doors and hurt was making her nearly insane with fear and frustration.

She'd spent what seemed an inordinate amount of time

giving the admissions clerk insurance and other information, when all she wanted to do was see her little girl.

A nurse had finally escorted them here to the waiting room, telling them a doctor was inside with Emma and would be out shortly to talk to her. That had been over an hour ago.

Trying to curb his own fears and frustration, Michael took the seat next to Angela and reached for her hand. It was icy and shaky. "Angela." He lifted her hand and kissed it. "Don't worry, I'm sure she'll be fine." He wished he'd sounded more confident, for Angela's sake.

"Then what's taking so long?" she demanded, surging to her feet. "And why won't they let me see her?" All kinds of thoughts and fears had run through her mind. Broken bones. Internal injuries. The school nurse had accompanied Emma in the ambulance and waited for Angela to arrive. She'd told them that Emma had fallen off the top of the monkey bars during recess. She and Barbie had been playing, and apparently Emma had slipped off.

The nurse had explained that from her initial cursory examination, she felt it best not to move Emma until the emergency medical technicians arrived. But she thought that Emma had a broken right arm, and perhaps a few other scrapes and bruises. Emma had never lost consciousness, even though she'd taken the brunt of the blow to her head and arm, but she *had* been badly frightened.

Knowing that only added to Angela's anxiety, but under the circumstances, she was pretty sure that was normal. Head injuries could cause very serious traumas, which only frightened Angela more.

"Michael." Dizzy with fear, her voice broke and she sank back down in the chair and reached for Michael's hand. "I...I don't know what I'd do if anything happened to her." Unable to contain her tears any longer, Angela buried her face in Michael's shoulder as sobs shook her whole body. "She's everything to me, Michael. Everything. I can't bear the thought of anything happening to her." How could she put into words what her child meant to her? She couldn't, she realized, especially not to someone who'd never had a child. The thought of losing a child was a fear that no parent should ever know.

"Shh, shh, it's all right," he soothed, draping his arm around her and pulling her close in spite of the fact that his own stomach was knotted with fear. "Nothing's going to happen to her, hon. I promise. Emma's a strong, healthy little girl. I'm sure she's going to be fine." He glared at the double doors, all but silently ordering the doctor to come to tell them what was going on. "She's going to be just fine, Angela." He kissed the top of her head and drew her even closer, not certain if it was for his comfort or hers. "I promise." He glared at the doors again, hoping—praying—this was one promise he'd be able to keep.

"Ms. DiRosa?"

Angela and Michael were on their feet the moment the doctor, with a smile on his face, pushed through the swinging doors. He was almost as round as he was tall, with bushy silver brows, silver hair and a kindly, weatherworn face filled with wrinkles.

"I'm Ms. Di Rosa," Angela said, stepping close to him. "How's my daughter?"

Smiling, the doctor patted her arm. "I'm Dr. Peterson, an orthopedic pediatric surgeon, and your daughter's going to be fine. A little sore, a little bruised, but she should be okay."

"Thank God." Letting out a breath, a relieved Angela sagged against Michael.

The doctor pushed off his blue surgical cap to scratch his silver head as his brows drew together. "She suffered a clean break through both growth bones in her right arm. We call it a buckle fracture and if you're going to break bones, that's the way to do it," he said. "We've set the bones and put a cast on the arm, but we're going to have to watch her and check the bones during the next several weeks to make sure they heal correctly."

Still feeling weak with fear, Angela nodded, clinging to Michael. "I understand."

"With growth bones, there's always a chance that they won't fuse together properly, and we'll need to go in and surgically rebreak them and then reset them properly so the arm grows properly." He touched her shoulder when her face paled. "That's a possibility, not a probability," he clarified with a comforting smile and a pat, "but something you should be aware of."

"I understand. Can I see her?"

"Yes, in a few minutes." The doctor smiled, then slipped his hands in his pockets. "She's got a pretty good-size goose egg on the side of her head where she hit the ground. Broke her glasses as well, I'm afraid."

"We can replace those," Michael said for both of them, tightening his arm around Angela and feeling his own rush of relief as the doctor went on.

"We've done some X rays and a few other tests and we don't believe she's got a concussion, but I'd like to keep her overnight just to keep an eye on her."

"Overnight?" Angela repeated. Emma had never been away from home overnight before. Not even for a sleepover. She didn't feel her daughter was old enough for that yet. Knowing Emma would be in the hospital overnight made Angela worry more.

The doctor nodded. "It's merely a precautionary move. She's going to be bruised and sore. She's got quite a whopper of a headache, I'm afraid, but I think she should be able to go home tomorrow if all goes well." He touched Angela's arm again. "I told her she's going to be quite a hit at school with her cast. She chose a neon-green glow-in-the dark one. Truly a fashion statement," he added with a chuckle. "Guaranteed to get as much attention as a new puppy." The doctor turned to Michael with an inquisitive lift of his brow. "I take it you're Michael?"

"Yes," he said, extending his free hand. "I'm, uh, Michael. Michael Gallagher. A friend of Emma and Angela's." He almost slipped and said *Lieutenant* Michael Gallagher out of habit. At that moment, Michael realized just how much of his life and his identity were tied up with his profession, just how little he had in his life but his job.

"Nice to meet you." The doctor shook his hand. "I have it on a good authority that you're the first person she wants to sign that cast."

Michael grinned, pleased and proud, and more relieved than he believed possible. "That's a deal."

"Now, Ms. DiRosa, I'll be back in the morning to check on her. The nurses will call me this evening if there's any change, but I don't expect any. We've given her a little something for the pain, nothing to knock her out because of the head injury, but just enough so that she'll be able to be comfortable. I'll be back in the morning to check on her and give you a list of instructions before taking her home."

Angela nodded, trying to commit everything to memory. But she was still so badly shaken, she knew she wasn't thinking carefully and was grateful for Michael's presence. "Anything else, Doctor Peterson?"

"Your daughter's had a bad fall and a bad scare, Ms. DiRosa, but it might help her if she doesn't see you looking quite so frightened," he said kindly, patting her shoulder. "Why don't you take a few minutes, go splash some water on your face and give your system a chance to calm down before you go in and see her."

Angela nodded as Michael glanced at her. The doctor was right, Angela looked as pale as the moon and terribly frightened. It was odd, since she'd always seemed so in control, but then, her child had never been hurt before. Instinctively, his arm tightened around her.

"I'll take care of her, Doc," Michael said, giving Angela's shoulder a squeeze. "I promise. I'll take care of both of them," he said firmly, meaning it.

"Good. Good." The doctor extended his hand. "It was nice meeting you. Wish it had been under different circumstances. If you have any questions, just give me a call."

"Will do, Doc," Michael said as the doctor turned and headed back into the examining room. "Thanks."

"She's going to be okay, Michael," Angela said in relief, turning into Michael's waiting arms and clinging to him. Now that the initial horrific fear had passed, she felt utterly drained, weak and totally exhausted.

"I know, hon, I know." He held her tight, burying his face in her hair, inhaling deeply of her wonderful scent, wanting nothing more than to make sure her and Emma were all right. Always. The knots in his own stomach were finally loosening and he took a deep, heartfelt breath of relief.

"Michael." Sniffling, Angela glanced up at him, her

heart full of gratitude and love, a love she knew was futile. "I don't know what I would have done without you today." She shook her head as fear shot through her again like an arrow, reminding her of those first, frightening moments when she learned that her child was hurt and that she couldn't get to her. "I...I...I...don't know what to say, how to thank you." Feeling helpless, she let her hands flutter impotently between them.

He kissed her forehead and drew her closer for a moment, just wanting the comfort of holding her. "Then don't say anything, Angela. It's just not necessary."

She nodded, realizing she had no idea what to say to him, how to thank him for what he'd done for her. Being there for her, supporting her was not something she was used to. From the day Emma had been born, she'd done everything alone; having someone here to lean on was a luxury she never thought she'd have.

"Now why don't you go wash your face off and then you can go in and see Emma." He needed a few minutes alone to get his own emotions under control.

"Don't you want to come, too?" Angela asked in surprise.

He grinned. "Well, yeah, but I'd thought you'd want to go in to see her alone first."

Angela shook her head. "No, Michael. I have a feeling nothing would make Emma feel better right now than to see both of us together." She wouldn't think about the fact that he was leaving. She simply wouldn't think about it when her mind and her heart were filled with so many other fears. She would simply enjoy and savor the fact that he was here with them for now.

He nodded, then grinned. "That would be great. Go wash your face and then we'll go see her together."

She nodded, then on impulse, leaned up and brushed her mouth against his, feeling a sense of completeness and comfort when her lips touched his. "Thank you, Michael, for being here."

She walked away before he could tell her there was no-where else in the world he'd rather be than with her and Em—here.

"I broke my glasses and I'm not gonna be able to go to my Brownie meeting tomorrow," Emma complained, fighting back tears as she snuggled deeper in the bed and squinted at Michael.

She had a goose egg sticking out the side of her head, making her look like she had a serious case of bed head, and a few bruises along her jaw. Her right arm was wrapped in a white cast wrapped in neon-green glow-in-the-dark gauze.

"Well, pint-size, I don't think you should be worrying about that right now," Michael said, gently brushing her hair out of her eyes. "Are you in pain?" he asked worriedly. He was sitting on the edge of the bed, trying not to worry about how pale and small Emma looked. Helpless, he thought nervously, when he'd never thought of her as help-less before.

Now she looked so small and fragile lying in that big white bed. She looked so tiny—the urge to scoop her up in his arms and hold her there forever so nothing could ever hurt again was so strong that Michael had a hard time not acting on his fears and feelings.

Emma frowned and then touched her cast with her free hand. "Not so much now." She scowled, pursing her lips as she lifted her fingers to the bump on her head. "My head hurts a little bit."

"Part of that is because you don't have your glasses on, Emma," Angela said, brushing a hand over Emma's. "Michael is going to go home in a little bit and get your other pair of glasses—you know, the emergency pair we keep in your desk?" Angela gingerly sat on the edge of her daughter's bed. "And as for your Brownie meeting, there'll be other meetings, honey."

"I know, Mama, but this was our Christmas meeting and I was supposed to bring the treats," Emma said glumly, fisting the thin white hospital sheet between her fingers. "And we were going to do our grab bag for presents."

"Well, pint-size, how about if I take your treats to your Brownie meeting for you? And take your grab bag present?"

Emma's face brightened for the first time since they'd entered the room. "Would you?" she asked hopefully, a grin tilting the corners of her mouth.

Michael laughed. If he'd known that taking some cookies and a present to a meeting would make her this happy, he'd have offered to do it right away. "Absolutely. I can get all the information about where it's at from Barbie's mother, can't I?" he asked, glancing at Angela who nodded. "See, honey, it will all work out."

"Are you gonna sign my cast?" Emma asked, lifting a hand to rub at her head, which was still hurting.

"Absolutely," Michael confirmed.

"Mama," Emma said solemnly, her voice soft and scared. "I have to stay here all night all by myself."

"No, honey, not all by yourself," Angela corrected with a smile. "I'm going to stay right here with you."

"Really?" Emma's face brightened.

"Really."

"Can Michael stay, too?" Emma asked hopefully, causing Angela and Michael to exchange glances.

"Actually, pint-size, I think I'd better go home and take
care of a few things there. But I'll come get you and your
mom first thing in the morning, how's that?"

"Fine." Emma was quiet for a moment, then turned to
her mother with a hopeful expression. "Mama, did you like
Dr. Peterson? I thought he was nice. *Real* nice," Emma
added with a roll of her eyes for emphasis. "Even if he is
old, he's not too cranky. And did you know Dr. Peterson
doesn't have a wife anymore 'cuz she died years and years
ago? He has kids, but he said they're all grown up, but he
likes kids, Mama, he told me he did. And he doesn't got a
wife now, so maybe—"

"Em." Angela's one-word admonishment caused Emma's eyes to widen innocently.

"What, Mama?"

Laughing, Angela shook her head. If her daughter was
back to matchmaking, she was probably going to be just
fine. Blessed relief surged through Angela and she smiled
at her daughter. "Try to get some rest." She tucked the sheet
and blanket tighter around her daughter. "And we'll discuss
this penchant you seem to have for matchmaking…later."

"Okay, Mama," Emma said, with a wide yawn. "But Dr.
Peterson really does like kids." Emma grinned as her eyes
drooped. "Even me."

Chapter Eight

The house seemed far too quiet and empty without Angela and Emma, Michael decided. Funny, he'd lived alone in his apartment for years and the silence and the solitude never bothered him. But here, at the inn without Angela or Emma everything seemed eerily off-kilter—especially him.

Unable to sleep and blaming it on sheer nerves and adrenaline pumping over the scare Emma had given them, Michael finally gave up trying to sleep and spent the night poring over his manuscript, checking it one last time, editing out sentences, words and even whole paragraphs in an effort to tighten it and make it a faster read.

Satisfied with the finished project, which he'd yet to tell Angela about, he collapsed into bed just near dawn, planning to catch, at best, a few hours of sleep. Exhausted, he fell asleep immediately.

Sunlight shining into his bedroom and the telephone woke him less than five hours later. After grabbing a quick, hot shower, he pulled on his jeans and a sweater and headed downstairs for some coffee.

"Morning," Jimmy grumbled limping toward the counter with the coffeepot, his cane clicking softly on the floor.

"Morning," Michael said, stifling a yawn and bending to scratch the dogs' heads. Bright sunshine filtered in through the windows, not that the sunshine could outshine Jimmy's clothing. Today, he was dressed in a bright red plaid shirt, with checks large enough to double as a checkerboard, and a pair of matching bright red jogging pants. The man certainly had a colorful wardrobe, Michael mused, trying not to grin.

"Fresh coffee in the pot," Jimmy said as he poured his own cup, then moved toward the refrigerator for some cream. "Angela called. Said they're waiting for the doc to come see Emma and release her. Once he does, she'll give a holler and you can go pick them up."

Michael nodded, taking a sip of his coffee and letting his eyes slide closed as the caffeine jolted his system. He had a million things to do before he went to the hospital to pick Emma up, and not a whole lot of time to do them.

"Understand Emma gave you all quite a scare yesterday," Jimmy said casually, as he set his cane down and pulled out a chair for himself.

"Yeah, she did," Michael said, dragging a hand through his hair and sitting down at the table, as well.

"You know, Angela, well, she's a fine, fine woman, and a damn fine mother." Jimmy dared a glance at Michael. "She's been taking care of that little imp all on her own since the day she was born."

"I know," Michael said carefully, realizing Jimmy probably had something on his mind. "She's done a wonderful job. She's a great mother."

"That she is." Jimmy hesitated, sipping his coffee. "And a good woman, as well. And let me tell you, it wasn't easy having and raising a child on her own. When Angela first arrived here, she was about to give birth and was sick with worry about how she was going to take care of herself and her baby. But she dug right in to help me without giving a thought to her own health or welfare." Jimmy sipped his coffee again. "She's an incredible woman, Michael, and deserves a helluva lot better than all the lies and deception she got from that ex-husband of hers, I tell you."

"Well, you're not going to get an argument from me on that," Michael confirmed, wondering if he should hunt up some of Angela's cookies for breakfast.

"I'm very fond of Angela," Jimmy said unnecessarily. "And of Emma. And not just because they're the only kin I've got left. No sir. There's just something special about the two of them." He looked at Michael steadily. "If you know what I mean."

"Yeah, I know what you mean," Michael said carefully, wondering where Jimmy was going with this.

"And I'd hate to see Angela or Emma hurt." Jimmy shook his head. "Especially since neither of them deserves any more hurt in their lives. Way I figure it, they've had more than their share."

"I couldn't agree more."

"Good. Good." Jimmy hesitated a moment, lifted his cup to sip his coffee and set it down quietly before turning to look at Michael. "I'm afraid they've both gotten awfully attached to you, Michael. And seeing how you're gonna be leaving soon, I figure that might be a problem for them."

"Jimmy." Michael waited until the old man glanced up at him. "I'd never do anything to hurt either of them."

"Good to hear, 'cuz I like you, son, and I'd hate to have to think about hurting you," Jimmy said casually. "And I'd have to hurt you if you hurt my girls."

Michael simply nodded solemnly. "I understand, Jimmy. Believe me. You love them and want to protect them. I can understand that. I feel the same way."

"Do you?"

Michael nodded again. "Yes, I do." Michael hesitated for a moment. "But I have no intention of hurting them."

"Well, son, I've lived long enough to know the path to hell is paved with good intentions."

"Jimmy?"

"Yes, son?"

"I love them. Both of them," Michael said simply. More than anything in the world. More importantly, he realized he needed them, as well.

"They know that?" Jimmy asked casually and Michael shook his head.

"No, not yet." He sighed deeply, twisting his coffee cup by the handle. "I've got a few things I've got to work out first before I tell them."

Jimmy nodded, then glanced at Michael. "And I assume one of those things you've got to work out is telling Angela you're a cop?"

Stunned, Michael simply stared at the old man. "You know?"

Jimmy nodded, then smiled. "Knew that first day when I had to come rescue you from the mutts." He chuckled at the look on Michael's face. "I spent twenty-nine years on the Green Bay Police Force before I retired, son, and I can smell a cop at forty paces."

"But you never said anything," Michael said in surprise.

Jimmy shrugged. "Not my place to say anything. Figured you had a good reason for not being honest with Angela." Cocking his head, he studied Michael for a moment. "You in some kind of trouble with the department son? Or maybe the law?"

"Lord, no," Michael said, dragging a hand through his hair. "Nothing like that." He hesitated a moment. "I'm an undercover narcotics detective. Have been for two years, although I've been on the force for ten. The press got a hold of my picture and plastered it all over the front pages of the Chicago papers, effectively blowing my cover. My commander ordered me to take a mandatory thirty-day vacation until all the hoopla dies down, hoping people will forget me and my face." Michael shrugged. "That's how I ended up here."

"Damn press," Jimmy said with such heat it made Michael smile. "They never think about the cops' lives they're jeopardizing in the zeal to get a story. And I'm sure they didn't realize by plastering your face on the front pages it might jeopardize your life, as well as your career."

"Exactly." Michael blew out a breath. "I've got some things to take care of on that end before I can think about a future with Angela and Emma."

"Well, that sounds like a mighty nice plan, son, but a word of caution. Angela is not going to be happy about being deceived, not with her history. Good reason and intentions or not, you're going to be facing an uphill battle son, and I can't say I envy you. No sirree," he added with a shake of his head.

"I know," Michael admitted, feeling a skitter of alarm. "But I'm hoping she'll be able to see I didn't do it to hurt her, but to protect her." He went on at Jimmy's perplexed look. "The last thing I wanted or needed was to have the press or someone a bit more sinister come looking for me up here. I would never want to bring the ugliness of that world here, to Angela and Emma's home, nor would I ever want to put them in any kind of danger. If no one knows who I really am, then they can't find me and certainly won't be looking for me in a small Wisconsin town."

"I see," Jimmy said. "And I understand 'cuz I been in your shoes. Let's just hope Angela understands."

"Yeah," Michael said, draining his coffee cup. "Let's hope she does."

Jimmy was quiet for a moment. "So you gonna be taking them both back to the city with you, then?"

Now Michael understood what was going on. Jimmy was afraid of losing Angela and Emma, afraid Michael would take them away from him.

"Jimmy." He laid his hand over the older man's. "This is Angela and Emma's home. I'd never, ever want to take them away from here or you. They're your family and they love you, Jimmy. Nothing will ever change that. And I'd never ask Angela or Emma to give up their home or the only family they've ever known."

Jimmy nodded, and Michael could see the relief in his face and his eyes. "Good. Because to tell you the truth, I don't know what I'd do without them." Jimmy drained his coffee cup, and Michael noted his hands were shaking. The old man pushed back from the table to get up and refill his cup. "You know, I was never blessed with a wife or children. Not that I didn't want them, mind you, I did." Jimmy stopped to refill his cup, reaching for Michael's and refilling it as well, before passing it back to him. "It just never seemed like the right time. And I always thought there'd be more time." He smiled as he headed back to the table with his coffee. "Funny, time seems to just get away from you and before you know it, you're old and sick and suddenly time has passed you by and you're all alone." He sat down heavily. "Not a good way for a man to live his life. Alone is good when you're young and foolish, and when you've got a career to fill all the empty hours. But I tell you, there's a lot more to life than a career, and there's been many a night that I've wished I had a woman by my side, someone to talk to and just share my day with, someone to comfort or bring little gifts to." Jimmy smiled woefully. "If I had it to do over again, I'd have spent less time planning my career and a lot more time planning my life. Too late you find out that one's far more important than the other."

"Yeah, I guess I've just begun to realize that," Michael admitted.

Satisfied he'd gotten his point across, Jimmy changed the subject. "So tell me son, how's that book of yours coming?"

Michael grinned. "It's finished. I finished it yesterday and did the final revisions last night."

Jimmy nodded. "Are you pleased with it?"

"Very," Michael admitted. "Angela read the first half and liked it."

"I know, that's why I asked, 'cuz she was raving about it. Think you might have a career in that field?"

"I don't know, Jimmy," Michael admitted honestly. "I hope so, but I just don't know." Michael glanced at the wall clock. "Jimmy, have you got any plans today?"

"Plans?" Frowning, Jimmy thought about it for a moment. "Well, nothing important. I've got to go into town to have another go-round with that butcher about Angela's meat order, but other than that, I've got nothing pressing, other than doing some prep work for the festival guests we're expecting. Why? You've got something for me to do?"

"Actually," Michael said with a grin, "there's quite a few things I need to do before I pick Angela and Emma up from the hospital and I was hoping you might be able to help me."

Jimmy grinned, then nodded his head and reached for his cane. "Well then, son, let's get a move on."

"Michael," Emma said with a grin, wrapping her arms tight around his neck as he scooped her up off her feet and into his arms. "You don't have to carry me into the house. I can walk," she added with a giggle, swinging her legs to and fro. "My arm's broke, not my leg."

"I know, pint-size," he said with a smile, hoisting her higher. "But a free ride never hurt anyone," he said as he stepped back to let Angela open the back door for them. Both dogs, who'd been snoozing by the door, immediately came to attention, barking as if an armed intruder was breaking in.

"Pipe down," Angela scolded as she turned to unzip Emma's winter coat. She glanced at Michael. He'd been acting awfully odd ever since he'd arrived at the hospital to pick them up, and she had no idea why.

Now that the initial crisis with Emma was over, she had to get back to work. With her first guests arriving tomorrow morning for the festival, she still had the enormous Christmas trees to decorate, not to mention some advance food preparation to handle. Time was short and she was starting to feel pressured; then again, she felt that way every year before the festival.

"Mackenzie! Mahoney!" Emma squealed, waving her cast-encased arm at them in greeting. "I missed you." The dogs circled Michael's legs, grumbling a welcome under their breaths. "Both of you." Emma giggled as Michael didn't bother to stop, but continued through the kitchen, kicking the swinging door open with his foot.

"Surprise! Surprise!"

Emma's eyes widened in shock as Barbie stepped forward from the group of little girls dressed in matching brown uniforms and matching brown beanies who had gathered around the Christmas tree in the living room.

"Hi, Em," Barbie said. "We decided to have our Brownie meeting here so you could come."

"You did?" Wide-eyed, Emma stared at the group of girls assembled, her heart all but dancing out of her chest. She turned to her mother. "Mama, did you hear? My Brownie meeting's going to be here."

"So I see," Angela said, her heart almost overflowing with love as she glanced at Michael, wondering how on earth he'd managed all of this by himself in just one night.

Her gaze went to the large Christmas tree in the corner by the game table. It had been bare when she left yesterday; that had been one of the chores she'd planned on doing yesterday, but hadn't gotten around to it because of Emma's accident.

Now it was brightly and gaily decorated to a tee, right down to the angel Emma had made last year as a tree-top ornament. Lights were strung and now lit, casting a festive glow to the room. Tears of happiness filled Angela's eyes but she blinked them away, not wanting to alarm Emma and spoil her joy of the moment.

"Michael arranged everything," Barbie said with a grin, slipping her hands into the pockets of her uniform. "My mom helped, too," Barbie added with a shrug. "Michael said since you couldn't come to the meeting, we could bring the meeting to you. And we did."

"Thank you, Michael," Emma said, planting a loud, smacking kiss on his cheek and nearly strangling him, she was hugging him so tightly.

"You're welcome, pint-size," he whispered, giving her a kiss on the cheek right back.

"I love you, Michael," Emma whispered, burying her face in his neck.

"And I love you, too, pint-size," Michael said for Emma's ears only, burying his face in the silk of her hair and saying a silent prayer that she was going to be okay. Until yesterday, until she'd been hurt, until he realized he could lose her, he hadn't realized just how much he loved this little tyke. Loved her with an intensity that both frightened and awed him.

"If Mama doesn't want to marry you, could I?" Emma whispered, hanging on to Michael tightly. His heart, once so carefully guarded, shattered into a million pieces.

"Oh, Em," he whispered, hugging her tightly.

"What do you say we get this meeting started?" Angela said as Michael carried Emma to the couch and set her down, grabbing a pillow for her to rest her injured arm on.

The girls gathered around Emma and were full of questions about her injury. The enormous fire in the fireplace shifted and crackled, throwing heat and warmth into the room.

No one had ever left school in an ambulance before, so Emma was the star of the meeting, fielding questions and giving answers.

"Does it hurt? Your arm?"

"Was it fun to ride in an ambulance?"

"Did you get to hear the siren from inside?"

"Does the cast hurt?"

"Can you move your fingers?"

"Did you have to get a shot?"

While the girls plied Emma with questions, Angela motioned Michael back into the kitchen.

"Michael, I don't know how to thank-you for for everything." Unbearably touched, she stood on tiptoe and kissed him. "For being with me yesterday when I was so frightened. For arranging all of this for Emma, for decorating all the trees, it's just...it's almost overwhelming." She couldn't remember ever when anyone had done so many thoughtful, wonderful things for her or her daughter. The love she felt inside for him seemed to blossom and grow, filling her with a sense of peace and joy she wasn't sure she'd ever known.

He slid his arms to her waist and drew her close. "Not so overwhelming when you have help, and your uncle Jimmy helped me this morning."

"Where is Uncle Jimmy by the way?" Angela asked, glancing around the kitchen.

"He...uh had an errand to run in town. I believe he said something about the butcher?"

Angela laughed. "That sounds about right." Unsure how to proceed, Angela merely stared at Michael. "You know, you are unbelievable, and I can't thank you enough."

"Uh, I think there's something you should know before you start thanking me."

"And what's that, Michael?" she asked with a lift of her brow.

"Well, I…uh…promised the little girls that if they had their meeting here, you'd make them lunch." Michael shrugged. "I can't cook so I guess—"

Angela chuckled, then shook her head. "Don't worry, Michael. You've done more than enough. I'll handle the rest." Regretfully, she stepped out of his arms. "Why don't you go upstairs and work? I know you haven't had much time the past couple of days."

He grinned. "Actually, I finished the book on Thursday night."

"Finished it?" Angela grinned at him as she slipped her apron off the hook by the back door and tied it on. "Michael, that's wonderful. I can't wait to read it," she said as she opened the refrigerator and started pulling out items to make lunch.

"I already printed out a copy of the whole thing for you." And he'd already sent the second half of the manuscript to Griffin, as well.

"Terrific. I may not get a chance to read it before our guests start arriving tomorrow, but I'm sure going to try."

"I'll go up and get it," he said. "That way, you'll have it whenever you have some time."

"Great." Angela watched as he pushed through the door. The girls' laughter filtered in through the open doorway for a moment, making her smile. It was good to hear Emma laugh again. It was good to have her home.

Home, Angela thought with a pang in her heart. If Michael had finished his book, she thought, turning on the burner on the stove, he'd be leaving soon. Refusing to allow her emotions loose, Angela blinked away tears and tried not to think about it. But she simply couldn't ignore the fact that now, with the book finished, it was time for Michael to go home.

And she had no idea what to do about it.

Chapter Nine

When the doorbell rang midmorning on Sunday, Angela was certain it was her first guest arriving for the festival. But when she pulled open the back door, she was surprised to find a rather sturdy-looking no-nonsense woman staring back at her.

"I'm Sadie James, the nurse at Emma's school." Clutching her pocketbook close to her body as if she had the Queen's jewels in them, Sadie surveyed Angela carefully from head to toe. "I've come to check on her. To see how she's doing." Sadie gave a nod of her dark head. "Hospitals have a tendency to make my patients worse, not better," she announced in a tone of voice that made Angela pray she'd never have the need for a nurse—sturdy or otherwise.

"How is she?" Sadie asked. She didn't wait to be asked to come in, but merely stepped over the threshold and around Angela and then glanced around with a nod, as if pleased.

"She's…she's doing wonderfully," Angela said, closing the door behind the woman, surprised that the dogs hadn't barked. Or moved. They merely laid where they were, peeking at the woman cautiously over their folded paws as if afraid to move or bark. Angela couldn't blame them.

"Good to hear," Sadie said with another nod of her head. Her black hair, spliced liberally with silver, was scraped back against her head into a chignon anchored right in the middle of the back of her head. Her dress was solid, mud-brown and as near to shapeless as anything Angela had ever seen. Her shoes, in the same shade of mud-brown, were low and sensible.

She wore no jewelry of any kind, nor any makeup, but she had an incredible complexion and enormous green eyes that complemented her coloring.

"I'd like to see her, if you don't mind?" Sadie said, making no secret of the fact that she was looking over Angela from head to toe. Self-consciously, Angela smoothed her hair down, fearing it was sticking up on end or something.

"Mind?" Angela swallowed. "No, no, of course not. I'll just go get her. Uh…um…would you like some coffee while you wait?"

Sadie nodded, setting her purse down on a chair and slipping her heavy black coat off, laying it across the table. "That would be lovely, yes, thank you." She smiled, and Angela found herself relaxing. The woman couldn't be too formidable if she could smile like that.

Angela hurriedly poured the woman some coffee, then

set a plate of homemade cookies out on the kitchen table. "I'll…uh…just…go get Emma," she said nervously, grateful to push through the doors and out of the kitchen.

She raced up to her room. "Emma, there's a Miss James here to see you. Sadie James. She says she's the school nurse."

Emma brightened, then bounced up from the floor where she'd been trying to color one-handed. "Ms. James is here?" she asked, her eyes glinting mischievously. "Great. But she's not here to see me, Mama. She's here to meet Uncle Jimmy."

Angela caught her daughter's good arm just as she tried to sail past her out of the room. "Whoa, whoa, whoa. Wait a minute, Em. What do you mean she's here to meet *Uncle Jimmy?*" Angela asked with a lift of her brow and a sinking feeling in her stomach.

Emma grinned, scratching her fingers where her cast ended. Her cast itched like crazy. "Ms. James and I was talking in the ambulance. And she's not married, but she likes kids, Mama." Emma giggled. "Like she said, she's gotta like kids because she works at a school full of 'em. Anyway, I told her about Uncle Jimmy, that he's not married and he likes kids, too. I told her to come over one day and she could meet him."

Angela was certain her heart was going to stop. "Emma Marie DiRosa, are you telling me you're trying to fix up Uncle Jimmy with that woman downstairs?"

"'Course, Mama. I thought it was a good idea, don't you?"

"Oh, Lord," Angela said, hanging her head and wondering how on earth she was going to get her uncle out of this mess. "Emma, why on earth did you ever think Uncle Jimmy would be interested in Miss James?"

Em grinned. "'Cuz she's not married, doesn't got any kids, but she likes them, and she's a champion checker player, that's why," Emma said as she skipped past her mother and out of the room.

"Terrific," Angela said, shoving her hair off her face. "That's just terrific." Following Emma downstairs, Angela tried to come up with a logical explanation to give her poor uncle. But when she got downstairs, she was stunned to see Sadie James and her uncle seated at the game table, talking and chuckling together as if they were old friends.

"See, Mama," Emma said, coming up to her and taking her hand. "I told you Uncle Jimmy would like her."

The doorbell rang again and Angela looked at her daughter. "Emma, is there anything else I should know? Any other unexpected guests I should be expecting?"

"No, Mama, why?" Emma asked, confused.

"Never mind," Angela said, going to the front door and pulling it open.

"Angie!" A barrel of a man, nearing sixty, engulfed her in a hug, lifting Angela up and off her feet. His wife whacked him on the back.

"Now Bart, you know better than to be picking her up like that. Your back ain't what it used to be." Bart's wife stepped in behind him, smiling at Angela. "Hello dear, I'm so glad to see you again." She kissed Angela's cheek, then glanced around the beautifully decorated room with a heavy, heartfelt sigh. "My, my, my, you've outdone yourself this year, Angela. The place looks lovely. I've been looking forward to the festival for six months."

"And to your fabulous home cooking for almost as long," Bart said as Angela took their coats.

Bart and Beverly Breech had been coming to the inn

every year for the Christmas festival for as long as Angela had been there. A retired police officer, Bart simply adored Emma, had watched her grow up and treated her like one of his own beloved grandchildren.

"Uncle Bart!" Emma cried when she saw him and ran to him. He caught her on the fly and swung her around.

"How's my little Emma?" He set her on her feet and drew back with a frown as he looked at her cast. "What happened here?" he asked, touching her arm gently.

"I fell off the monkey bars at school," Emma announced with a grin. "And I had to go to the hospital in an ambulance. I broke my arm twice and then at the hospital the doctor gave me a shot and put a cast on my arm. I had to stay overnight and just came home yesterday. The school nurse, Miss James, she rode with me in the ambulance and we talked. She's not married and she likes kids and she's a champion checker player."

"Is she now?" Bart said with a laugh, patting Emma on the head. He was so used to Emma's machine-gun style of speech he never batted an eyelash. "How long does she have to keep that on, Angela?" Bart asked, nodding toward Emma's cast.

"Six to eight weeks," Angela said, going to the guest closet to hang up their coats.

Bart whistled. "Is she hurting any?" he asked with concern, making Angela smile.

"Not anymore. It was touch and go the first night, but she's doing very well now."

"Glad to hear it." He grinned, then patted his rotund belly. "Real glad to hear it." He sniffed deeply. "What's that I smell? Something wonderful I bet."

Angela laughed. "I made your favorite beef Bourguignon for dinner, Bart." She hooked her arm through his. "And I've got your rooms all ready, as well." She glanced at her daughter, who was hovering near the game table watching Jimmy and Sadie's spirited checker game. "Emma?"

"Yes, Mama?"

"Would you run up and tell Michael we have guests? I'll need him to get their bags out of the car."

"Okay, Mama." Emma skipped off, taking the steps two at a time.

"Got yourself some new help this year, Angela?"

"Just for the festival," she said. "Normally, we just hire college kids from town, as you know. But this year we lucked out, and one of our guests, a writer who's been here for a month working on a book, offered to help out in exchange for his room and board. It's worked out well," Angela said as she led the Breeches up the stairs and toward their room. "Michael's been a godsend this year with everything that's happened."

"A writer?" Beverly said, pressing a hand to her heart and fluttering her eyes dramatically. "That sounds so romantic. What does he write?"

"Mysteries. I guess you could call them cop dramas," Angela said with a smile. "But you can ask him yourself."

The door to Michael's room opened and, holding Emma in his arms, he stepped out into the hallway.

Angela started to make introductions, but Bart cut her off. He stepped forward, closer to Michael, and squinted at him.

"Michael Gallagher, is that you?" Bart squinted at Michael again and then took a step closer, extending his hand.

"Bart Breech, I don't believe it. I haven't seen you since

your retirement party," Michael said with a grin, taking the older man's hand and shaking it. "Retirement's been good for you," he said, looking the man over. "How are you doing?"

Too late, Michael realized that his past had followed him up here and Angela was about to find out the truth about him—about who he was and what he did. And more importantly, that'd he'd been dishonest with her and with Emma.

"Fine, fine, son. How are you? And all your brothers?"

"Everyone's doing just great."

"Do you two know each other?" Angela asked carefully, totally confused, looking from one man to the other.

"This here's no writer, Angela. This here's one of the best undercover narcotic detectives Chicago's ever had. Yes, sirree, me and Michael worked a few cases together, and I gotta tell you, he's one of the best."

"Narcotics detective?" Angela said, struggling to understand what she was hearing. "Michael, is that true?" she asked, totally confused. "Are you really an undercover detective?"

He had no choice. He wasn't going to lie right to her face. "Yes, it's true," he admitted and saw the hurt flood her eyes like a tidal wave. He wanted to grab her and hustle her off somewhere where he could explain, talk to her alone, let her know that this wasn't what she was thinking.

He could see by the color flooding her face that she'd already damned him. Damned him in the same category as her ex-husband.

"I'm a Chicago cop, a lieutenant in the narcotics division and I've been working undercover for the past two years."

"Have you been working undercover here, the past

month?" she asked, aware that even to her own ears her voice sounded strained. The moment Michael admitted who he really was, admitted that this whole time he'd been lying to her, deceiving her about who he was, she felt the blood drain from her face and her body, leaving her cold and shivering. So cold she could feel it all the way to her marrow.

"No, Angela." He started to reach for her, but watched her step back a bit and saw the warning flash in her eyes. "No," he said again. "I've really been on vacation."

She merely nodded as if she hadn't quite believed him. "I see," she said, rubbing her hands up and down her arms and wishing her heart weren't pounding so loudly in her chest, her ears. She wasn't certain it was possible to actually feel a heart break, but what Michael's admission had done was cause this incredible pain inside—so incredible that it had to be her heart breaking.

She'd trusted him, believed him. Even knowing about her background with her ex-husband, he'd still chosen to lie and deceive her. How on earth could he do such a thing? How on earth could he live with himself? And more importantly, why would he do such a thing to her and to Emma?

Emma. Oh, dear God. Emma had no idea that Michael wasn't at all what he'd been pretending to be. She had to protect her little girl, had to protect her so she didn't get hurt any more than necessary.

"Emma, come here, baby." Angela lifted her arms, took her daughter from Michael and tucked her comfortably against her hip.

"Angela." He hesitated, not wanting to talk in front of anyone. "We need to talk."

She forced a smile. "Yes, well, I'm afraid it will have

to wait." She nodded toward the Breeches who were still standing in the hallway, watching them both carefully. "As you can see, I've got guests to take care of." She glanced at Emma with a smile. "And a daughter to see to. If you don't mind, Michael, I'd appreciate it if you could get the Breeches' luggage while I get them settled."

He hesitated just a moment. "Sure. I'll be happy to."

"Good seeing you again, Michael," Bart said with a grin and a wave as Michael made his way downstairs.

Forcing a smile, and determined not to let the devastation or desolation show, Angela dug in her pocket for the keys to all the guest rooms. "Why don't we get you settled in? Then you can freshen up a bit before dinner."

It was after ten before everyone had left or retired to their rooms and Michael couldn't wait to talk to Angela alone. He knew she was still in the kitchen because he'd been watching, waiting for a moment to be alone with her.

Gathering his courage, he pushed through the doors. The kitchen light was off, but the stove and night-lights were on, casting the room in a faint, hazy golden glow.

"Angela, I want to talk to you."

Trying to ignore what his presence was doing to her heart, Angela glanced up from the Crock-Pot, where she'd been assembling ingredients to start a pot of soup for tomorrow. She planned to let the soup simmer overnight so that she would have one less thing to bother with the next day.

"Yes, Michael, I imagine you do," she said coolly. "I'd like to talk to you, as well."

Carefully, she set her spoon down, then turned to him. The look on her face all but broke his heart.

"I'd like you to leave. First thing tomorrow morning."

"Leave?" Panic surged through him and he clenched his fists. "I can't leave, Angela, not until you give me a chance to explain." He took a step closer, but stopped when she lifted a hand in the air. "Please, at least give me that."

"Michael." She took a deep breath, struggling to contain the tears that had been threatening to fall since she'd learned who he really was. "There's really nothing for you to explain, now is there? You lied to me about who you were, didn't you? You said you were a writer when, in fact, you're really not. You're a cop, is that correct?"

"Yes, but—"

"You deliberately lied to me, deliberately chose to deceive me and my daughter for no good reason?"

"Yes. No." He shook his head. She was confusing everything. "Yes, I lied to you and deceived you, Angela, but trust me, I had a very good reason."

"Trust you?" she repeated with a lift of her brow, her heart aching. "I hardly think you're in a position to ask me to trust you or anything you say. After what's happened, what makes you think I'd believe anything you have to say?"

"Because I'm going to tell you the truth—"

"I see. Now you're going to tell me the truth? So the truth is something you pull out whenever it's handy, but otherwise it's just as easy to lie?"

"Of course not," he said. "I lied to Emma and you, Angela, in an effort to keep us safe."

She stopped and stared at him. "To keep us safe? Well, I don't know how to break this to you, Michael, but Emma and I have always been safe, except, of course, when we learn that people we love and trust have lied to us and deceived us."

"Do you love me, Angela?" he asked quietly. From the

surprise on her face, he knew she'd said the words without even thinking about them.

"That's beside the point," she said stiffly, realizing she was not about to admit her feelings for him, not now. How could she love a man she couldn't trust? And hadn't she already been through this heartache once before?

"No, Angela, quite frankly, I think it is the point."

She shook her head. "It doesn't matter, Michael. Doesn't matter at all, because you can't love someone you can't trust, and clearly I can't trust you."

"So what you're saying is that rather than hear me out and give me a chance to explain, you'd rather just turn your back on me and what we could have together."

"You can't have a relationship based on lies, Michael. And that's all we've apparently had between us. Lies and deceit, Michael, and in case you didn't understand this before, please understand it now. I could never love a man who can't be honest with me."

Taking a deep breath, Angela forced herself to battle back the tears that were threatening to fall.

"Now I'd like you to leave. First thing in the morning," she clarified, forcing herself to keep her tumultuous emotions in check. "Knowing about my past, knowing how much I value honesty, you chose to deliberately lie to me and my daughter, to deliberately deceive us without giving one thought, or one consideration to our feelings."

Inhaling deeply, Angela slipped her fisted hands into her pants. "I find that reprehensible, Michael. Not to mention inexcusable."

She turned away from him and picked up her spoon. "I've already told Emma that you're leaving in the morning. I'd appreciate it if you'd be gone by the time she gets up. She's been hurt enough by this. I would prefer she not be hurt any further."

"That's it, Angela?" Angry at himself and the circumstances, Michael stepped closer, aching to touch and hold her. "That's the end of us?" He couldn't bear the thought that he was losing her and Emma. He simply couldn't bear it.

"There is no us, Michael," she said, forcing the words out. "There never was, since you were never honest about who and what you were."

She laughed, but the sound held no mirth. "I thought I was older, wiser, smarter, but apparently I'm not. I blindly believed everything you said simply because of my heart."

She shot a glance at him, her courage bolstered. "But believe me, I've learned my lesson now. Leave Michael," she said forcefully, biting her lip to hold back the tears. "We have nothing else to say to one another."

In spite of the fact that during festival week Angela was so busy she barely had time to think, she was utterly, absolutely miserable without Michael. His leaving had left a hole the size of a crater in her wounded, broken heart and she couldn't bear the thought of facing the days without him.

And it was no better for Emma. With school out for Christmas, she simply moped around the house, grousing and complaining about being bored. Angela knew all that was really wrong with her was that she missed Michael.

If it wasn't for Sadie who'd become a daily visitor to the inn, Angela was certain Uncle Jimmy would be moping around, as well. He and Sadie seemed to have hit it off perfectly, spending most of their time together, much to Angela's surprise.

With Christmas Eve just a day away, on Sunday afternoon—when the last festival guest had finally departed, when the last meal had been prepared and when the inn was finally once again blissfully quiet—Angela decided to take the rest of the day off.

Jimmy and Sadie had taken Emma to an early evening movie and then out to dinner, an early Christmas present, and Angela wanted nothing more than to have a little quiet time to herself.

Exhausted and heartsick during the past week since Michael had left, she'd been able to keep herself busy enough so that she hadn't had time to think about Michael or about her aching heart. The disappointment she felt was so acute, so deep, she couldn't even begin to put it into words.

She had no idea why he had chosen to lie to her about who he was—she'd never given him a chance to explain. But then, would that explanation really matter, she wondered, as she ran hot water so that she could indulge in a bubble bath.

Reasons wouldn't matter, she realized dully, rubbing a hand over her heart as if she could erase the ache. It didn't matter why he'd deliberately deceived her, what mattered was that he *had.*

And she simply couldn't trust someone who would deliberately do that. Not just to her, but to Emma, as well, she thought, getting out of the tub as the water cooled. After drying herself off, Angela wrapped herself in a warm terry-cloth robe, pulled on a warm pair of socks and then headed to her own bedroom for some downtime.

Curling up in her own bed, she grabbed Michael's manuscript. So many things had happened so quickly that she hadn't had a chance to finish it and she wanted to find out how his story ended.

Three hours later, Angela finished Michael's manuscript and she knew about his father's death, about his promise to himself never to put his own family through that pain, knew about how important his work was to him and about the family tradition he felt duty-bound to honor in memory of his father.

She knew and understood all of it now; what she didn't understand was why he hadn't simply told her the truth in the beginning.

"Mama?" Emma crawled into her bed and nudged her awake. "Mama, wake up. It's Christmas Eve day and we've got lots to do."

"Em, what time is it?" Angela asked on a groan, turning over and pulling the covers up higher.

"Five-fifteen," Emma said brightly.

"In the morning?" Angela all but croaked. So much for having a day off.

"Yep. And guess what?"

"The Cubs are gonna win the pennant?" Angela mumbled, making Emma laugh.

"No, Mama. It's snowing. Big, fat flakes of snow are everywhere."

"What?" Angela bolted upright in bed. She had a million things left to do today and the last thing she needed was to deal with another snowstorm. On Christmas Eve she and Emma had a tradition—they spent the day together, going into town doing last-minute errands and delivering cookies to the nursing home. Then they cooked a very special dinner together, lit a fire, opened a few presents and then watched the Christmas movies they rented. At midnight, they'd go to services at the local church to cap off the evening.

"It's snowing, Mama. Lots and lots," Emma said, gleefully bouncing off the bed and crossing to the window to look out. "See. Isn't it pretty?"

"Gorgeous," Angela mumbled, climbing out of bed to look at the snow herself.

"Uncle Jimmy said that we're supposed to get another whopper tonight," Emma said. "So does that mean we can't do the stuff we planned?"

"No, sweetheart. It just means that we'll have to get started early, before it gets too bad out." Angela frowned for a moment. "But if it does get bad, we might not go to services tonight because of the roads."

"That's okay, Mama. Can we still go into town and to the nursing home and will you still help me wrap presents? I've still gotta wrap Michael's present."

"Emma." Angela turned her daughter to face her. "You know I explained to you that Michael went home?"

Emma nodded solemnly. "But that doesn't mean he's not coming back, Mama," she said worriedly, making Angela's heart ache.

"Well, maybe we can wrap Michael's present and mail it to him. What do you think of that? He won't get it before Christmas tomorrow, but I'll bet he'll get it the next day."

Emma shook her head stubbornly. "No, Mama. I don't want to mail it. I want to give it to him." Emma's chin lifted. "I know you said he went home because he had to be with his family for Christmas, but I still think he's coming back. I love Michael, Mama, and he said he loves me, and I don't think he would miss being here for Christmas."

Angela sighed, wondering how on earth she was ever going to get her daughter to understand about Michael. She glanced at her daughter's face and felt a stab of pain in her heart. How could she get Emma to understand when she herself didn't understand?

She didn't know, but unless she wanted Christmas ruined for Emma, she was going to have to figure out a way to make her daughter understand. Or else.

"I appreciate your inviting Sadie to Christmas Eve dinner, Angela," Jimmy said that evening as he brought the good silver candlesticks into the kitchen where Angela was setting the table.

It had been a hectic day, made more complicated by the snow that had, indeed, kept falling, but she and Emma had managed to get everything done. She had to admit she was grateful to be home and out of the storm now.

"Uncle Jimmy, this is your home," Angela said taking the candles from him and setting them on the table. "I'm happy that you're finally inviting your friends over." Angela tried to smother a smile. "You seem to get along really well with Sadie," she said casually. Considering Jimmy and Sadie had been spending every waking minute together since they'd met indicated that more than a friendship was developing, but Angela wasn't about to point that out to her uncle.

"She's a wonderful woman, Angela, just wonderful." He winked, then straightened the tie he wore only on Christmas Eve. It was bright green and lit up and flashed, all the while playing "Jingle Bells." "And I haven't been this happy in a long time."

"Good." Angela stood on tiptoe to kiss his cheek. "I'm thrilled for you, Uncle Jimmy."

The front doorbell rang, sending the dogs into a manic

round of barking. "Stop that you two," Jimmy groused, grabbing his cane. "It's just Sadie, Angela," he said, smoothing down his hair. "Would you go let her in while I get out the wine?" Looking sheepish, he shrugged. "I forgot to open it to let it breathe."

"Sure." Wiping her hands on her apron, Angela went to the front door, followed by the dogs. She pulled open the door and stared, her heart taking one giant leap, as if it would come right out of her chest.

"Michael." She was surprised she'd found her voice. He looked fabulous, she thought, even with snow covering his topcoat and dusting his black hair. She swallowed hard. "What…what are you doing here?"

"It's Christmas Eve," he said quietly. "And I had to bring Emma her present." His smile widened. "Besides, your Uncle Jimmy invited me for dinner."

"Dinner," she repeated dully. He nodded.

"Are you going to let me in, Angela? Or do I get to stand out here in the cold all night?"

"Come in," she finally said, opening the door wider to let him pass. The dogs immediately encircled him, licking his hands and jumping up on him, grumbling and growling deeply under their breaths in welcome.

"Hi, boys, yeah, I missed you, too," Michael soothed, going down on one knee to pet them both and then burying his face in their soft coats. "I missed you a lot."

"Michael!" Emma squealed from the top of the stairs. She hurried down two steps at a time, jumping down from the last one to dash across the room and leap into his arms. "You came, you came. I knew it. I knew you'd come, didn't I, Mama?"

Pointedly ignoring her daughter's question, Angela quietly shut the door behind Michael, desperately trying to hang on to her composure. Seeing him again made her realize just how much she'd missed him, how much she loved him. And she didn't want to remember, didn't want to feel those things.

Grinning, Michael swung Emma around in a circle. "Hi, pint-size. Merry Christmas."

"Merry Christmas, Michael." She wrapped her skinny arms around his neck and kissed his face. "We missed you. All of us, right, Mama?" she said, turning to her mother, who pointedly ignored the question.

"How's your arm?" Michael asked, frowning down at the cast.

"Better," Emma said, grinning happily. "Dr. Peterson says a few more weeks and I can get the cast off." She scowled. "It itches like cooties."

Laughing, Michael set her down on her feet and put the shopping bag full of gifts he'd brought down on the floor next to her.

"Emma, would you take these gifts and put them under the tree?"

"Emma." Angela's voice stopped her daughter. "After you do that, please go upstairs—"

"Angela. I need to talk to you. Both of you." He glanced at Emma who stood between them looking from one to the other. "Emma, can you find the two presents addressed to your mom in that bag, please?"

"Michael—"

"Angela, please indulge me for a minute." He shrugged out of his topcoat and laid it over the couch. Underneath, he wore a beautifully tailored pin-striped blue suit and a white shirt and tie that only added to his attractiveness and made Angela want to throw herself in his arms.

"Here they are," Emma said, handing them to her mother.

"Michael, this wasn't necessary," Angela said, feeling more than a bit embarrassed.

"Yes, it is. Open them."

"Now?" Angela said in surprise.

"Now," Michael confirmed.

"But we normally don't open presents until—"

"This is a special occasion, right, Emma?" He wasn't above using Emma to help his cause right now, knowing how much was at stake.

"Right. Come on, Mama, open them," Emma encouraged, eyes shining brightly.

"Okay, fine, I'll open them." Angela went to the couch and sat down, setting the packages on her lap. She lifted one. It was very small and almost flat. When she opened it she merely stared at it. "A plaid bow tie, Michael?" she said in surprise. "You bought me a bow tie?"

"Yep," he said with a grin, sitting down next to her and pulling Emma onto his lap.

"Okay," Angela said, willing to go along for the moment.

"Open the next one," Michael encouraged.

Angela reached for the other box. It wasn't much bigger, and she ripped the paper off to discover a stuffed fish.

She looked at it for a long moment before lifting it out of the box to show Emma. "It's a fish. A stuffed fish," she said quizzically.

"Ah, but not just any fish, Angela. It's a goldfish."

"Okay, it's a goldfish. Thank you very much," she said, with such excruciating politeness that he laughed.

"You don't get it, do you?"

"I don't even know what it is I'm supposed to get," she admitted.

"Angela." He reached for her hand, refusing to let her pull away. "Listen to me for a minute. Please?"

Knowing Emma was watching, knowing it was Christmas Eve, knowing she'd not been fair to not listen to his explanation before, Angela nodded.

"Fine, Michael. I'll listen to you." Primly, she folded her hands in her lap, laying them over her fish.

"When I arrived here, I was on a mandatory thirty-day leave from the department because the day before, I'd rescued a toddler from a busy street. The press picked up the story and my picture was plastered all over the front pages of every Chicago newspaper, threatening not just my work but my life, as well." He hesitated, not wanting to say too much to frighten Emma. "The press was on my tail, looking for me for an exclusive interview and I had to get out of town and hide for a while. That's how I ended up here. I was afraid if I told you who I was and what I did that it would somehow put you and Emma in danger, not just from the press but from any of the more sinister elements I've dealt with over the years."

"You didn't tell us who you were because you were trying to protect us?" she asked in surprise.

"Maybe not a very good reason in your mind, but then you haven't worked with the people I have during the past ten years. My cover was totally blown, Angela, and I had no idea who might be looking for me. I couldn't take a chance on someone maybe following me or bringing that kind of element here with me. If no one knew who I really was, then no one would be looking for me here. It's that simple."

"And you didn't think you could have told me that, Michael?" she asked, trying not to let the tears form. Her emotions were zigzagging every which way, a confusing mix of love, need and hope.

"You're asking me to make a judgment based on hindsight, and that's not fair, Angela. I did the best I could at the time with the knowledge I had. All I knew was that Michael Gallagher, undercover cop, had his cover blown and had to disappear for a while. And that's all I did." He hesitated. "I never meant to lie or deceive you, but at the time, when I first got here, Angela, it never occurred to me that I'd fall in love with you and Emma."

"You…you love me?" she asked hesitantly, her heart swelling with a mixture of joy and fear.

"I love both of you," he said, nuzzling his face in Emma's hair.

"I told you, Mama. Didn't I tell you Michael loved me?"

Angela laughed, brushing away her tears. "You're right Emma, you did tell me."

"Michael." Angela hesitated. "I finished your book." She allowed herself to reach for his hand. "I know now that book really is about you and your experiences, isn't it?" she asked quietly. He nodded, then blew out a breath. "I know about your father, Michael, and the promise you made to yourself about never putting your own family through that." Angela took a deep breath. "So I know that loving us is still a problem for you."

"Actually, it's not, Angela." He hesitated, searching her eyes, grasping for hope. "I resigned from the force yesterday."

"What?" Stunned, she shook her head. "Oh my word! Michael." She shook her head. "I don't understand. I thought…from your book I thought you loved being a cop."

He grinned. "I did," he admitted. "But I found there's something else I love even more. Tons more." He touched her face. It had been too long, way too long, since he'd touched her. "You and Emma."

"Michael?" Emma said, glancing up at him and turning his face down so she could look in his eyes. "Does this mean you're gonna ask my mama to be your wife?"

Michael laughed. "Well, I think I already did." He nodded toward the stuffed fish and the bow tie. "It seems to me, Angela, that you told me that you needed a husband like a goldfish needs a bow tie. I think if you put that tie on that fish there, you'll see that he really needs it. Just as much as you need a husband and Emma needs a father, and I need both of you." He grinned, then glanced down at Emma and whispered loud enough for Angela to hear. "You have no idea how hard I had to shop to find a stuffed fish and then a bow tie that would fit around it!"

"Does this mean I'm going to get to have a sister or a brother now?" Emma asked in excitement, trying not to bounce herself right off of Michael's lap.

"I think you'll have to ask you mother about that, honey," Michael said with a smile. "But it sounds pretty good to me."

"But Michael, what will you do? You don't have a job now because of us, and—"

"Angela, apparently I didn't lie to you when I told you I was a writer." He laughed. "Maybe I didn't quite believe it myself at the time, but apparently I really am a writer."

Her gaze searched his face and she squeezed his hand, excitement and joy rushing through her. "What happened, Michael?"

Shaking his head in disbelief, he laughed. "Griffin's been in New York most of the week meeting with editors. He's gotten several offers for the book, nothing outrageous, but more than enough to support a family, and one of the publishers is making noises about making this a recurring series, with the main character tackling a new case in each book."

"Oh, my God, Michael, that's wonderful." Now, the tears did come and Angela let them. She hugged Michael tightly. "I'm so proud of you."

"So," Michael said. "Seems like I am officially a writer now, which means I'm going to need a nice, quiet place to write and live." He glanced around. "And since I seem to do my best work here, I was wondering how you'd feel about sharing your life, your love and everything else with me, Angela?" He hesitated. "That is, if you can forgive me."

Her eyes slid closed for a moment and she remembered something else he'd once told her—Big risks. Big Rewards.

"Yes, yes, Michael. I can forgive you and I will marry you," she cried, throwing her arms around him and holding him tightly. There was no bigger reward in life than to marry the man you loved, she thought, holding him close.

"I'll marry you, too, Michael," Emma said with a grin.

"You will, huh? Okay then, it's time for the real Christmas presents. Emma, reach your hand into my pocket, my right pocket."

Clapping her hands in glee, Emma reached her hand into his right pocket and pulled out a small white jewel box.

"Ah, that one's yours, Emma."

"Mine?" Her eyes rounded. "Can I open it?"

"Yep," Michael said, sitting back and draping his arm around Angela to hold her close.

Slowly, holding her breath, Emma opened the little box and then sighed. Loudly. "Mama, Mama, look. It's a ring. A green ring to match my cast." She yanked it out of the box.

"It's an emerald, Emma, and it's also a promise to you that I will love you and take care of you all the days of my life."

"Like a regular daddy?"

"Just like a regular daddy," Michael confirmed as he slid the tiny ring on Emma's finger and brought her close to kiss her forehead. "*Your* daddy, Emma. Forever."

"Now, Emma, reach into my other pocket." She did, pulling out the small, velvet box. "That one is for your mother." Emma handed it to Angela, who nervously opened it.

"Michael." Her breath rushed out at her when she saw the beautiful diamond solitaire on the simple gold band. "It's beautiful," she whispered. Tears blurred her vision.

"Angela," he said, taking the ring out of the box and slipping it onto her finger. "This is my promise to you, as well. I promise to love you, take care of you and always, always be honest with you—no matter what—for all the days of our lives."

"Oh, Michael." Sighing with relief, with love, Angela wrapped her arms around him, holding him close, letting the hope and the love she'd held inside of her for so long go free.

"Now," Michael said, pulling back from Angela. "I do believe someone said something about dinner." He sniffed, then grinned. "I've missed your cooking, Angela, and everything else about my family."

"We're you're family, Michael, and you're ours. Forever," Emma announced, looking at her ring. "Right?"

Michael pulled Angela to her feet and scooped Emma up in his arms. "You're right, Emma. We're a family, and I hope you don't mind, but tomorrow the rest of the Gallagher family is going to come up here to meet all of you if that's all right?"

Angela slid her arm around his waist. "That will be

wonderful, Michael. I can't wait to meet all your brothers and your grandfather and your sister."

"Michael?" Emma asked with a frown, still looking at her ring.

"Yes, honey?"

"How many brothers do you have?"

"Five," he said with a laugh as he headed toward the kitchen, looking at her suspiciously. He remembered the last time she'd asked him this.

"Do they like kids?" Emma asked with a mischievous glance. "Your brothers, I mean. 'Cuz my friend, Josh, he doesn't got a daddy, either. His daddy died and he's just got a mother. A real pretty mother, but no brothers or sisters, and he really wants a brother bad." Emma rolled her eyes. "Real bad. And so I was thinking—"

"Em?"

"Huh?"

"Stop thinking!"

"Yeah, but what about your brothers?" Emma asked with a scowl, her mind already plotting and planning.

"Honey, I've got *my* family. As for my brothers, well, hon, they're on their own!"

* * * * *

Don't miss Sharon DeVita's next book,
RIGHTFULLY HIS,
coming to Silhouette Special Edition
in December 2004.

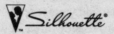

Coming in December 2004

SILHOUETTE *Romance*®

presents a brand-new book from
reader favorite

Linda Goodnight

Don't miss...

THE LEAST LIKELY GROOM, #1747

Injured rodeo rider Jett Garret meets his match in feisty
nurse Becka Washburn who only wants to tend to his
wounds and send him on his way. But after some intensive
at-home care, the pretty single mom realizes that this
Texas cowboy is slowly working his way
into her heart.

Available at your favorite retail outlet.

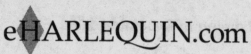

COMING NEXT MONTH

#1746 HER FROG PRINCE—Shirley Jump

In a Fairy Tale World...

Bradford Smith needed to get rid of his scruffy image...
fast! And buying a week of feisty beauty Parris Hammond's
consulting services was the answer to his prayers. But would
the sassy socialite be able to turn this sexy, but stylistically chal-
lenged dud into the stud of her dreams?

#1747 THE LEAST LIKELY GROOM—Linda Goodnight

Clinging to a dream, injured bull rider Jett Garret would do *anything* to return to the circuit—and the pretty nurse he'd
hired was his ticket back to the danger he craved. But after
spending time with Becka Washburn and her young son,
Jett soon found himself thinking the real danger might
be losing this ready-made family.

#1748 THE TRUTH ABOUT PLAIN JANE—
Roxann Delaney

In a big curly wig and fake glasses, Meg Chastain had come to
Trey Brannigan's dude ranch to write the exposé that would
make her career. Meg knew the Triple B meant everything
to Trey...but she was out to prove that she could be
so much more....

#1749 LOVE CHRONICLES—Lissa Manley

Sunny Williams was on a mission—to convince oh-so-sexy
Connor Forbes that her holistic methods would enhance his
small-town medical practice. The dishy doctor had never
valued alternative medicine, but as Connor spent time with
the beautiful blonde, he began to discover that he might
want to make sweet Sunny his partner for good!